STEEP STEPS TO NOWHERE

And Other Short Stories

R K Baratan

MINERVA PRESS
NEW DELHI
MIAMI LONDON

STEEP STEPS TO NOWHERE: *And Other Short Stories*

ISBN 81 7662 209 5

First Published 2001 by
MINERVA PRESS
13 Palam Marg
Vasant Vihar
New Delhi – 110 057

Printed & bound in India
for Minerva Press (India) Pvt. Ltd.

STEEP STEPS TO NOWHERE

And Other Short Stories

For Chandra, always with me,
&
Shriram, Shrikanth, Shrinath & Sridev
who believed in me
even when it was difficult to believe.

Contents

Mashed Tomato

They first saw each other while walking early mornings. Cursory nods gradually turned to mumbled greetings, and then, when unavoidable, they fell in step. Each, pushing sixty, was wary of getting close to strangers too soon. In the beginning, the only bond was the zeal for walking, and their love of dogs.

Ram walked his pedigree Doberman – a rippling sheen of black and tan, thigh-high, with cropped tail and ears. Arrow was fiercely protective and would go for anyone who as much as pointed a finger at Ram. He needed careful handling. Sunder's tiny Apso, a showpiece of canine beauty, shimmered in her silken silver-white splendour. Both were stunners – one for its restless, brute strength, the other for its picture-postcard charm. A striking contrast of beauty and the beast. Strangely, they did not even snarl at each other, and this gradually brought their owners together.

They could not say if it had taken weeks or months to talk about each other. Ram had retired as Agricultural Consultant to the World Bank. Shareen and he had just one son, away in New Zealand on a UN assignment. He had married a Punjabi girl.

'No. No children,' he smiled. 'Not grandfathered yet.' Both laughed.

Sunder had spent a lifetime in journalism, and had edited two of the best English dailies in the country. Shyla and he had only a daughter, a freelance fashion-columnist. Modelling for expensive soaps, designer clothes, cellular phones and what not, she was also a familiar face to subscribers of elite magazines.

'Very much single. You know how girls are these days,' Sunder tried to mask his pride. 'Sniping at the bold and the beautiful one day, savoir-faire before a battery of studio cameras the next morning. Could scare the stuffing out of a guy who wants to pop the question.' More chuckling by both.

Ram asked Sunder over for a drink, and Shareen insisted he and Shyla stay on for potluck dinner. The wives found they had a lot in common. A few days later, Sunder had the Ram Chanders over, and while the men drank Scotch, talking of dog-care, share market woes and jokers in politics, Shyla showed Shareen her daughter's photographs.

Back home, Shareen sighed, 'How I wish Jacky had not allowed that Punjabi girl to hook him.' And that said it all. Soon, they were meeting for bridge two to three times a week, and it was as though they had known each other for years.

Ram and Sunder gradually built a cache of stag jokes, each with an abbreviated code. One of them would pop a catchword, and they laughed together. The wives, who knew their foibles, would smile indulgently.

One of their coded jokes was 'Mashed Tomato'. When they were by themselves, they called her 'The Creature' or just 'Mash'. She lived in the small house on a lonely side road, ideal for walking. The building was set well back from the gate, with trees and unkempt bushes all over the compound. From the terrace, a thatched sunshade slanted downwards, covering almost the entire front of the house, masking every window from the road. It was dingy, with dim electric bulbs adding to its macabre gloom. The gate was always locked from inside.

The house faced the high rear wall of the school compound across the road, and that made it even more drab. The road, spattered with patches of grass and dusty shrubs on both sides, made it ideal for the dogs to sniff around.

'The very thought of sighting Mash makes them…' Ram said, imitating a dog lift its hind leg, and they laughed like kids sharing a dirty joke.

'Makes them want to…' added Sunder, and they exploded. Since they walked early mornings or late evenings, with hardly anyone on the lonely road, they could drop all inhibitions with puckish abandon.

Gradually, they identified the others in the house they christened, the 'Faceless Prison'. There was the sloppy middle-aged man, his forehead smeared with *vibhuti*, always bare above the waist, except for his sacred thread. They nicknamed him 'Ashley'. His wife with diamond earrings and nose studs, and an assortment of heavy gold bangles, waddled around in garish silk *saris*. They often saw her vigorously scrubbing pots and pans in the trough on the side of the house. She was named 'Scrubby'. A skinny, old lady, with thick post-cataract spectacles tied with a dirty string behind her ears, lolled on the steps of the house, chanting the name of every god in Hindu mythology. She became 'Her Holiness.'

The last of the 'obnoxious foursome' was Mash. Short and stubby, she was always bundled neck to ankles in heavy nine-yard *saris*. It was as though her head had been squeezed in a giant clamp, leaving a swollen, reddish scar from above her forehead down the entire left half of her face. From a distance, it looked like an over-ripe tomato trampled carelessly on the ground.

Since the dogs lingered on the road outside the house to sniff at the shrubs, they often saw the girl squatting on her haunches outside the house. She had a strange way of peeling coconut fronds to make brooms. She would pinch each with her fingernails, and pull out the leafy part with the other hand. And the broomstick invariably came clean as though smoothed by a sharp blade. To trim the broomsticks to size, she just bit through them.

'Mash technology', they chuckled, 'claws and jaws'.

The only other person they ever saw in the house was the man who was there off and on to pluck coconuts. They were amazed when they once saw Mash easily catch a coconut he dropped as though it was a mere rubber ball.

Neither spoke to their wife about the girl, and she remained their private joke. They knew the ladies were at times irritated, when they overstretched their Mash yarns.

The Sunders decided to take their summer break that year, in the hill resort where they had a time-share. Shareen asked them over for dinner the day before they left, to give Shyla more time for last-minute packing.

They were in high spirits that evening, particularly because they played husbands Vs wives rubber of bridge, the men tippling Goan Fenny in iced coconut water. Shareen had made a special dish of layered *ghee*-rice, and when it was brought to the table, sprinkled with deep-fried onion shreds and browned cashew nuts, it almost looked like a Christmas cake. After dinner, Ram opened a bottle of French Cognac. The ladies sipped Port. When they left, Ram was crestfallen. 'I'll miss the blighter a full ten days,' he grumbled, as he got ready for bed. Brushing her hair, Shareen agreed.

It must have been three or four days after the Sunders had left. Arrow was particularly restless that evening, though Ram had allowed him to tear around the bungalow over an hour. He kept pawing Ram's slippers, a clear sign that he wanted to go out.

'I think he badly wants a walk, Ram,' Shareen pleaded. He decided to take the short route. As usual, Arrow tarried outside the Faceless Prison. The road was already dark, and there was just one dim bulb behind the thatched shade of the dreary house. Slowly, Ram sensed someone looking at him just inside its gate, and was surprised to find it was Mash. As his eyes adapted to the darkness, he saw that her *sari* had come partly undone, and lay coiled at her feet. He could see her breasts, full, firm, push through her unfastened blouse. They seemed luminous.

Ram was drawn to the gate like an automaton. He seemed to have lost control of his senses, his feet, himself. As he neared the gate, the rest of her *sari* slid to the ground, and he saw that her skirt was tied loosely below her navel. Her waist was slender, and her hips full, rounded.

He was breathing heavily, and as he edged closer, he heard the gate being unlatched. She stood just inside, her body open to him. Only her face was tilted, veiled by the thick wavy hair that streamed down her shoulders. She was much taller than she had looked in her cumbersome *saris*. Arrow's leash slipped from his hand as Ram moved towards her in a frenzy, scanning the house and the road to make sure there was no one around.

He felt her coarse grip tighten around his wrists as she drew his hands to her breasts. He trembled when he first touched, and then fondled them. She threw one arm around his neck, drawing him close. Her hair smelt fresh, sweet. Tense and hard all over, his whole body throbbed with yearning as his hands caressed her silk-smooth body. With her free hand, she tossed her *sari* over the gate, screening it from the road. Ram tugged at the tape that held up her skirt, and it dropped to her feet. She shrugged off her blouse and was naked. With both her hands on his shoulders, she pushed him to his knees, clasping his face to her soft belly. She kept rubbing her thighs together in erotic sensuousness, as Ram fondled her slender legs.

The hands on his shoulders suddenly tightened, and Ram winced as her nails cut into his flesh. Looking up, he was startled by her scarred face, contorted with craving, her mouth open. She slid her hands under his arms and with fiendish strength yanked him off his feet, lifting him towards her as though he was a rag-doll. Ram felt choked as her embrace tightened like a vice, and he groaned before his lips were smothered by her open mouth.

In a flash, Arrow was crouching near the gate, his teeth bared, growling menacingly at the girl. A terrified screech pierced the silence, and Ram was flung almost half way across the road by a vicious push. The gate snapped shut just before Arrow lunged, barking furiously, his paws clawing the top of the gate. The girl had vanished. Ram stood up, quickly tidied his clothes and pushed back his hair, before grabbing Arrow's leash. He walked home swiftly.

'You took a long while, Ram,' Shareen said, without looking up from the magazine she was reading in the sit-out. She wore a pale-green cotton *sari* with a low-neck sleeveless blouse, and her tiny manicured feet were propped on a padded footstool.

'I'll be back in a moment,' he said, and locked Arrow in the kennel. He soaped his arms and face in the bathroom and brushed his teeth. Just in case the animal smell of that girl lingered, he changed his T-shirt and walking shorts, and slipped into loose white kurta-pyjamas. Shareen was extremely sensitive to smell, and yards away would scent anything unusual. He went to her, leaned over and kissed her full on her mouth, hard, fierce, demanding. She was startled, and tried to push him away.

'What's the caveman up to?' she teased. But it was clear she was pleasantly surprised. He lifted her towards him, and though she tried to resist when he hurried her to the bedroom, Ram knew she was feigning. He was in a frenzy of desire, and she let him have his way, shameless, untiring. And she responded willingly, even when his demands turned erotic. Sated, spent, they fell apart, realising the bedroom door was open. And yet for a long while, they lay still. She took his face gently in both her hands and kissed him tenderly on his lips, before quickly rolling away, leaving him naked on the bed. When she came back from the bathroom, he watched her deftly snap on her bra, before slipping into a flimsy nightie. She had just finished touching up her face, when the bedside phone rang. It was Sunder from Kodaikanal.

'How's life out there, Yaar?' he asked.

'Tops!' Ram drawled, still naked, drowsy. Shareen muffled a girlish giggle.

'It's raining out here, and this place is miserable.' Sunder's voice was slurred. 'I've worked my way through my third large drink, and it looks like I've not even started. And can you believe this? Shyla is just back from a walk in the rain. The strange ways of women.'

Ram smiled as he handed over the receiver to Shareen, who talked to Shyla. He hardly heard what she spoke. The overwhelming relief at having escaped from the maniac strength and lust of that awesome creature flooded through him. It had been a near thing.

He dawdled over just one tall cocktail before dinner, and when they went to bed, after watching a late night movie on TV, he was a very tender lover.

'Something's so different in you, Ram,' Shareen whispered, cuddling close. 'Whatever it is, it's lovely, darling.' And exhausted, they fell asleep in each other's arms.

The Sunders were back, but during their morning walk, Ram always hurried past the Faceless Prison, restraining Arrow from growling at its gate. They never saw the girl anywhere.

'Mash seems to have gone underground, or is it under someone,' Sunder joked. Ram just nodded.

Soon, they were set to leave for New Zealand on their annual holiday with Jacky and his wife. From there, they would stay awhile in Australia, and then visit friends in Fiji for a week, before they returned.

Shareen called Shyla as soon as they returned and was shocked when she said Sunder was back home from the hospital. 'He is better now,' Shyla said. 'All the bandages have been removed.'

'What bandages?' Ram heard Shareen ask. They talked at length, with Shareen sounding increasingly baffled. When she finally put the receiver down, she seemed aghast.

'It's unbelievable, Ram,' she said.

'What happened?' Ram was deeply concerned. 'I must look him up. Was he in intensive care? I never knew he had a bad heart.'

'Shyla suggests we keep away for some time. He does not want any visitors. Not even you.'

And then it came tumbling out, hazy, almost mysterious. Sunder had gone to walk the dog rather late one evening. About an hour later, Shiny came running back alone, dragging her leash. Shyla panicked and rushed the cook and watchmen, who finally found Sunder sprawled on the lonely road, outside that dilapidated house behind the school compound. His face and neck were covered with blood, his clothes in a mess. Though conscious, he couldn't speak. His mind seemed to have blanked out.

'She thinks he could have been hit by a vehicle, and dragged some distance,' Shareen continued, 'Shyla says there were lacerations on his body, neck and face. His lips were almost mangled. He could have fallen face down. Thank God, his eyes have not been affected. He was incoherent, and even now remembers very little. Temporary amnesia from a terrifying experience, the doctors told her.' Ram remained silent.

'Shyla says strangely some injuries looked like teeth or nail marks. They wonder if he could have been attacked by a dog. I can't believe that, because Sunder was always so good with dogs. He could even manage Arrow. And yet that's what the doctors too suspect. Perhaps, it could be that one or more dogs attacked Shiny, and Sunder would have tried to protect her, and that could have provoked an unexpected attack on him, and in the confusion a car could have knocked him down. They have completed plastic surgery,' Shareen continued, 'and almost corrected the injuries on his lips, face and neck. The rest of the scars, she says, will be hidden by his clothes.'

When they were in bed that night, Shareen sounded miserable.

'The dreadful incident seems to have changed Sunder and Shyla so much.'

'Shyla sounds so bitter.' Shareen was anguished. 'She says Sunder has become a recluse. Refuses to meet anyone. Drinks far too much. She seems so unhappy. Says, he is no more the warm, witty person he used to be. From the carefree couple they were, they now seem withdrawn, and in some way, secretive.'

Long after Shareen was asleep, Ram lay on his back, staring at the ceiling. In the silence of the night, he heard Arrow barking fiercely, and then growl himself to silence. He felt reassured, safe. He looked at Shareen's face, so trusting, so serene in sleep, and leaning over, gently kissed her forehead.

A Few Weeks With Priya

With his flair for appearing important, he breezed into the international terminal with his wife, even though visitors were banned. Shami carried Priya, as he helped Roopa check in. Then came the flurry of kisses and hugs. And more hugs, kisses and tears, as his wife coaxed Priya into his arms, and kissed Roopa goodbye.

Relieved when the fuss was over, he carried Priya to the security check-in, bemused by female farewell rituals. Roopa was going to join her husband in the United States, and for all her grumbling about the long flight alone with the baby, he knew she was yearning to be with Ranjan, after four long months in India. And yet embracing and kissing, and of course the tears came so easily to women.

Priya seemed to sense what was happening, and would not immediately go to Roopa. She clung to his neck, her cheeks pressed to his. The security guard gave him an indulgent smile as she helped Roopa with the baby's carry-bag and the folded stroller.

'No hurry,' she said, 'There is time.'

But he already had enough. The struggle to fit in Roopa's baggage in the car, unloading the boxes on the airport trolley, shoving each through the baggage screener and on to the weighing counter, and then carrying Priya up to the security-check entrance. He was more vexed than tired, and wanted to get back home. He had enough, even though Priya, their only grandchild, had been with them just four months.

'Let's go,' he told Shami as soon as he was back in the passenger lounge. But she would not budge, dabbing her eyes with a wisp of a handkerchief, and blowing her nose into a paper napkin. And no, she did not want a Pepsi. She would sit there till the plane took off, and that was over an hour and a half away.

He knew talking to her would not change her mind. Picking up a Pepsi, he sauntered to the large well-lit tank in the lobby, and watched the fishes dart around. It was weeks since he had cleaned his aquarium. Another job he would have time for, now that Priya would not jam the clear-cut schedule he set for himself each day.

Clear-cut. Everything about Ram was clear-cut. He could look back on his clear-cut life with satisfaction – with a touch of pride. He had done well in studies, joined a reputed company, swept Shami off her feet, and then despite the odd setbacks and hiccups, steadily gone up the corporate ladder, to retire as Chairman & Managing Director. He refused the offer of an extension, to settle in the lovely farmhouse they had built, now nestling among the trees Shami and he had planted years ago.

Ranjan, their only child, had gone to the best of schools, played collegiate cricket, majored in management, and decided to make a career for himself in the United States. Roopa was all they could expect of a daughter-in-law, and now there was Priya to round off a well-ordered life.

But even more importantly, he was still active – lean, greying with dignity. And Shami could, at times, pass off as Roopa's elder sister. There was a touch of grey at her temples, and her body was not as firm as it was, but with a stern diet and long morning walks, she was still lovely. He could look at her across the room during a party, and feel the excitement of driving her back at night.

From the beginning, Shami and he had agreed to split time for their distinct interests, He had his prize-winning Doberman they called Arrow, an exotic aquarium, his exclusive club where he played a good game of billiards, and a hideout behind the garage, in which he could work with his tool-set, mending and making all sorts of things. And though he rarely had more than a drink or two a day, his guests knew his connoisseur's collection of liquor.

Shami wrote a popular cookery column for a women's magazine, played rummy thrice a week, and kept a house that did them proud. The parties they hosted, always with something special on the menu, were the talk of' their elite circle of friends.

One thing they always did together was gardening, and Shami was well known for her collection or bonsai and he for the orchids he nurtured. Life after retirement had slipped into a groove of delightful routine, with everything falling in place. Three years after Ranjan and Roopa were married, they had Priyadarshini. 'She's as pretty as a Barbie doll,' Roopa's mother said, when she called from the States.

'So you've turned Yankee,' he teased, before handing over the phone to Shami.

Seven months later, he was there, when Ranjan and Roopa stepped off the escalator. He had managed special permission to be in the international passenger lounge. He took Priya from Roopa. Yes, she was very pretty.

He remembered Ranjan when he was a baby. Priya had the same shock of straight jet-black hair, but her long fingers and rich colour came from Shami.

A month later, Ranjan went back, to take up the new top management position he had bagged. Roopa and Priya would spend four months in India with them and her parents.

The first few weeks were a lark, with Priya easily sitting up and then speeding along on her hands and knees. Seat-belted into a stroller, he wheeled her out mornings and evenings, masking his pride when passers-by ogled. When anyone tried to touch Priya, she leaned towards him, her tiny hand reaching out for his finger. The moment she touched him, she felt safe.

Life remained the same, except that Shami turned a fulltime grandma. She stopped her morning walks, and it was now the bearer who brought him his bed tea.

'Madam's in the baby's room. Shall I pour your tea, sir.'

'No, I'll manage,' he tried to sound unconcerned.

As soon as he got back after his morning walk, Arrow, for all his protests, went straight to the kennel built behind their bedroom. He could not be allowed to tear about, with Priya crawling all over the house.

Priya crossed her milestones faster than normal babies, and was soon on her feet, with everyone in the house clapping when she managed to wobble a step or two. Shami and Roopa squatted on the floor, as Priya, arms stretched out, toddled unsteadily from one to the other. She loved to walk between his knees, holding his fingers with her hands. Once she could manage on her own, she seemed to take over the house.

The ashtrays, antiques and curios, tastefully arranged on the display shelves and low tables were put away. He came home one day to see the peg-tables looking like skeletons. With their glass tops removed, they were now placed as barricades to prevent Priya from going anywhere near the low-level electric switch-boxes.

Shami got him to fix slide-in baby-gates at the foot of the staircase, the kitchen door, and his sunk-in bar, tastefully set apart from the living room by an arrangement of indoor plants. The pots too were shifted in a few days. Then, Shami told him she would roll up the carpet the next day, and that it would have to go into the loft.

'Soon we will be living in barracks,' he retorted.

'Ram, Priya needs more space to move around safely,' she said.

'Why can't you keep her in a couple of rooms?'

'Ram,' she almost snapped. And it ended there.

Their first big row was when Shami refused to go to the annual club dinner, where they were toasted year after year, as the 'For Each Other' couple.

'Priya has to be bathed, and I must help feed her,' she said.

'Why can't Roopa do it?' he asked.

'Of course, she can. But I want to help her,' Shami was firm.

'And when she is away in the States?' he almost taunted.

'As long as Priya is with us, I want to do all I can for her. These dinners come and go.'

'But Shami, everyone will ask why you didn't come. It will sound silly, if I say you are sitting at home feeding the baby,' he argued.

'And what is wrong in that?' Shami shot back.

'But…but…'

'You tell them I'd much rather help care for any baby, leave alone Priya, than waste time in the club, where no one bothers about 'For Each Other' couples, the next day.'

'So, you think…'

'Enough of this, Ram. So long as Priya is here, please leave me out of all this…'

He went alone, was miserable, had more drinks than usual, and woke up the next day with a headache.

As he drove Shami home, after Roopa's flight had taken off, he was a bit guilty at his sense of relief. Shami and he could go back to their life together. Babies were wonderful so long as there were two oceans in between, he thought.

Though they slept late, he woke early, and lazed in bed. A pall of uneasy calm seemed to have fallen on the house. Shami used to bring Priya to their room early mornings, and almost immediately she wanted to be bounced on his knee, clapping her tiny hands, squealing with delight, till she carried her away so that he could have his morning tea.

In a sleek housecoat, Shami came in with the tray.

'A penny for your…' she smiled.

He looked at the bedside clock.

'They should have left Hong Kong for the long haul to Los Angeles,' he said.

'Oh, Roopa will manage.' Shami poured his tea.

'But there was some problem with Priya's right ear,' he reminded her, as he took his cup.

'Oh, babies have some small problem or the other. Priya will be all right,' Shami said, sipping her tea. 'And now you buzz off with Arrow. I've a whole lot of work on my hands.'

He shaved and tidied, and walked the long route, coming back sweat-soaked and hungry.

Shami had almost put the house in apple-pie order – the peg tables, the carpet, curios, even the indoor pots. She was in the sit-out, trying a new flower arrangement.

'Have you called Ranjan?' he asked,

'What on earth for?' Shami looked up. 'He knows the flight schedule.'

'But in case…'

'Oh, leave them alone, dear. They will manage better than we ever did,' she teased, snipping a twig a little short, pushing a sprig a bit to the left. Ram was surprised. Shami had dropped everything just to help change Priya's diaper. Even the club dinner. Oh, well!

He stepped into the guestroom on his way to the shower. Priya's teddy bear was propped on the baby-cot. The yawning emptiness of the room seemed to sweep into him. He backed away into the living room, and for want of anything to do, started edging the peg-tables just right. Priya had always shoved them around, just as Ranjan, when he started walking.

He paused at the photo-album cabinet, and opened one. Yes, there was the picture he had taken of Ranjan pushing the wicker chair. Shami came in with the flower arrangement and looked over his shoulder. He leaned towards her, but she pushed him away gently.

'You haven't bathed yet,' she grimaced. 'And it's time I washed your walking shoes.'

He showered, slipped into a T-shirt and corduroy slacks and went to the dining room. He had been looking forward to these leisurely breakfasts with Shami – just the two of them, with the bearer bringing in his eggs fried the way he liked them, while Shami buttered the toast. The newspaper lay fresh beside his plate. Priya had always messed it up.

After breakfast he checked the orchids, and picked up the wrench. The garden tap needed tightening. Perhaps, the washer would have to be changed. Normally, this would have been the first thing he would have done after breakfast. But today he was not up to it.

He snapped open his digital diary and scanned world-time. It would be another three hours before Roopa and Priya landed in Los Angeles. Ranjan had arranged with a friend, to bring Priya's morning feed to the airport. But would he?

'Shami, don't you think we should call that chap in LA and remind him of Priya's morning feed?'

'Why are you so restless, Ram?' Shami came in. 'Ranjan would have organised that. And even if he does not turn up, Roopa said she would get something from the hostess. I've made a list of things that need to be fixed. I think pushing Priya around in the stroller, playing gran'dad, has made you lazy.'

Playing gran'dad? Ram looked up sharply. Shami was just teasing, but the words kept bouncing in his mind. He could not shake them off. Playing... had he really been playing gran'dad? Had she said it only in jest?

The feeling of relief when he drove Shami home after the plane had taken off came to his mind. Shami stricken, huddled at the outer edge of the seat, looking away from him. But she had bounced back to her old self the next morning, while he was still numb with guilt. Both his joy when Priya was with them, and the relief when she left, suddenly seemed hollow. It annoyed him, but he could not shake himself free.

He picked up the wrench, and it did not take him long to fix the leaky garden-tap. He cleaned and oiled the wrench as usual, before he put it back in its slot on the tool-board and washed his hands. He carefully examined the aquarium. There was no need for immediate cleaning. He removed the dead underwater plants, adjusted the air-vents, and wiped the front glasses clean. The fishes darted up as he dropped pellets of feed in the tanks.

He rifled through the newspaper, but soon dropped it on the side-table. He used to hide his irritation, when Roopa brought Priya for her mid-morning stroll before he finished reading the newspaper – a sacred chore, soon after breakfast. But today it lay unread, on the side-table.

He could only think of how Priya would dive towards him, one finger in her mouth, pointing with the other hand at the stroller. And her impatience when he took time to snap on the seat-belt. Every outing was an adventure in discovery for her. The cow, a puppy, the crows swooping from perch to perch – she pointed at them gurgling with delight.

He eased himself into the leather armchair, sinking into its deep comfort. His mind wandered to the day they bought it. They had been married for just a few weeks, and were setting up their first home in the one-bedroom flat he had leased. Till then, he had stayed in the company's guesthouse.

'Buy a new set of furniture?' Shami asked when he told her he had saved enough to buy whatever she wanted.

'I want you to have the best, and I have the dough.' There was a touch of pride in his words.

'Oh no, Ram, that's not the way to do it. Let us hunt around. It's so much fun.'

And off they went, through narrow alleys, poking around the second-hand shops. Shami located the chair in one of them, behind a pile of discarded wooden panelling. She put her finger to her lips, asking him to be silent. The man asked three hundred rupees. And then the way she pretended that the last thing she wanted was that chair! He was baffled.

'Three hundred rupees, bhai? For this junk? Come, come, you must be kidding. Here is something on which my cat would not curl, and you want three hundred rupees. Ram, let's go, Bhai wants to steal our money.'

But the man followed, saying okay, okay, Madam, you mention a price. And then to his utter surprise she had gone back, pointing out one defect after another, saying every time. 'And you want three hundred rupees, Bhai? Three hundred rupees?' Finally, the man buckled, and they bought it for a hundred rupees. A few weeks later when he came home, he found Shami in jeans and a T-shirt he had discarded, furiously polishing the chair.

'Goodness, what have you done with it, Shami?' he was astonished.

'Nothing much. A few springs had to be changed, and I got it re-stuffed. The leftover floor polish is good enough to give it a new lick. The leather is superb.' She made a couple of soft cushions of the same colour as the leather. And later, she found a leather-upholstered foot-stool and got it done up. They were the centerpiece of their drawing room arrangement, and everyone who came admired the chair and its comfort.

And Shami's refrain was, 'Oh, Ram has a way of picking the right thing. Lucky me.' And he smiled, and left it at that.

Now positioned in his hideout, with sturdy peg-tables on either side, it was still his favourite chair. Their old colour TV was set across the room, and over a beer he could watch his favourite sports programmes, when Shami and her friends played rummy in their designer-furnished drawing room.

Coming to think of it, everything about Shami bore this stamp. She knew just what she wanted, knew how to get it, at the price she was willing to pay, and then where to get it done up. And always it was, 'Oh, Ram! He has a way about these things. Lucky me.'

Slumped in the chair, Ram was forced to admit that never once had he denied the credit she so gracefully heaped on him. Not once.

He must have dozed. He woke up to find the curtains drawn, the volume of the TV turned down, and the newspaper neatly folded on the peg-table. He stretched, got up, and shuffled into the house, calling for Shami.

'Just a moment, Ram,' her voice came from the kitchen. Sitting at the dining table, he sorted through the mail, pushed aside the sales letters and scanned the bank statement. The dividend vouchers had been credited, and also his pension. Normally, the first thing he would have done, would have been to put all unwanted papers in the trash bin, and neatly file the bank statement. But today he just leaned back in the chair, leaving them scattered on the table. An envelope fluttered to the ground, but he made no attempt to pick it up.

'I've made your potted roast just right, dear. Would you like a beer as a starter?' Shami asked as she came in and picked up the envelope. She looked at him closely, and when he said nothing, placed her hand on his brow.

'You tired, Ram?' Her voice was anxious. He shook his head.

'Shanti called to remind us about cocktails at her place this evening,' she told him. 'Said, Suri the cartoonist was coming, and wanted to make sure you would be there. Said, only you could keep him interested and sober.'

'Why don't we just stay at home today?' he yawned. 'Ranjan and Roopa are sure to call.'

'But they will leave a message on the answering machine, and we can call back, Ram. You always liked going to Shanti's parties. And I could wear the green hand-embroidered *sari* you bought me when we shopped for Roopa. I've got it pressed. But if you do not feel up to it...'

'Of course, we must go,' he said, putting his arm around her waist. And then, as though from a distance, he heard himself asking, 'Have you really been happy with me, Shami?'

She sank to her knees beside his chair, her eyes searching his face. 'What made you say that, Ram?' Her voice was soft and concerned.

He wanted to come clean. He tried. Struggled with himself. But he just could not say a word. And what hurt the most was knowing he never would.

One Went Home

The truck must have reached within minutes of the head-on collision. The driver and the cleaner extricated the two bodies from the mangled car and van, and rushed them to the nearest clinic. The doctor directed them to the super-speciality hospital.

The trauma care team, alerted by the doctor, swung into action. Blood-soaked clothes were scissored off to assess injuries. There was a card in the wallet of one of them.

Salina was in the lawn doddling over evening tea when the phone rang. In minutes, she drove into the hospital. Through the window of the trauma ward, she saw the two inert bodies side by side, swathed in bandages, blood and saline bottles hooked into each.

She recognised Mukul from his immaculately manicured toenails. He was always so finicky about them, even though his toes were squat, and he was flat-footed. The toenails of the other were unkempt, coarse.

Her thoughts were so wayward, that she barely heard what the doctors said. Except a hazy realisation that Mukul was serious and anything could happen.

Mukul's colleagues and the Agency's doctor had also reached. Someone gave her a cup of hot coffee. Special nursing had already been arranged. They persuaded Salina to go home at eight in the night. A senior colleague and the Agency's doctor would stay in the hospital and keep her informed.

'What about the other er… man?' Salina asked haltingly. She couldn't get the ugly toenails out of her mind. Nor the gracefully arched feet. The duty doctor looked at the

Agency's doctor. After a pause, he said, 'Drunken driving.' Salina looked from one to the other, and again at the two bodies in the trauma ward. She tried to speak.

'I have seen the case-sheets. There will be no problems for the GM. We got through to the chairman, and he will be flying in earliest possible,' the Agency's doctor told her.

'The other?'

'They don't know yet.'

From the telephone number painted on the van, the police contacted the owners. He was identified as Vasu, but being a casual driver, they did not have his current home address. It was when his picture was flashed in the local papers the next day that Saroja came to know of the accident. She tore into the hospital, and the security staff had to struggle to stop her from rushing into the trauma ward.

'What else can you expect from that drunken monster's wife?' The special nurse was peeved.

'Amma,' Saroja wailed, falling on her knees before Salina. I always warned him. But would he listen? Needed to keep going, he argued. Beat me when I refused to go buy it for him. And now see, what he has done. I'm going to be a widow. I know that. But why should an angel like you suffer because of his madness? Oh, Amma, please forgive him, forgive him, and me...'

The uncombed hair, the tear-streaked face, the coarse, crumpled *sari*. Salina took it all in first glance. Only Saroja's teeth seemed perfect. Each so tiny, well-aligned, sparkling white.

The ward boys tried to drag her away, but Salina restrained them. She asked the special nurse to give her a cup of coffee, and seeing the way she gulped it, gave her the sandwiches remaining in the hamper. She wolfed them. Salina took a hundred-rupee note from her purse and gave it to Saroja.

'Oh Amma, you are a goddess,' Saroja started weeping louder, clutching Salina's feet. 'And to think my useless husband has widowed you,' she chanted in a singsong voice.

The night nurse asked the ward boys to remove her to the verandah so that she would not further distress Salina.

The doctors did a head-scan on Mukul and found two hairline cracks on his skull. But his pulse seemed stable. They would have to wait and watch.

'He seems to be standing it remarkably well,' one said. 'He is strong. A real fighter.'

'The other?' Salina asked hesitantly.

'His company says he was just a temporary driver, and they can't take any responsibility. They have asked us to shift him to the government hospital.'

'No,' Salina's voice was low but firm.

'But madam, I talked to our lawyer, and he said that if we don't...' the Agency's doctor persisted.

'If he has no insurance cover, then Mukul will pay. We... I... will pay,' she said.

'Oh, no, Madam. The chairman called to say that everything should be done to your entire satisfaction.'

'Please, let it be for both of them,' Salina pleaded. 'Only don't let his wife know. She thinks the hospital is paying for his treatment.'

Vasu was given a total scan, and they found that he did not have any head injury. All were below shoulder level. A lung had been pierced by a broken rib, and it may need surgical correction. His chances were fifty-fifty.

Mukul and Vasu continued to share adjacent beds.

Bit by bit, Salina pieced together what had happened that fateful day. Mukul had reached the office very early. He found the entire team waiting. The presentation was in the forenoon.

Everyone knew the stakes involved. It was one of the juiciest advertising contracts – a giant multinational entering the Indian market. Every top ad agency in the country was in the chase for this mega account. The competition had brought out the best and the worst in the fiercely competitive ad world.

What happened in Mukul's firm was unprecedented. The chairman overlooked its high-profile executive director, and asked Mukul, the GM, if he would take charge of the presentation. Mukul agreed, provided he could choose a taskforce, and the chairman's immediate response was 'yes'. In a couple of days, his hand-picked team was ready, raring to go.

Mukul unleashed a demoniac energy the Agency had never known before. For three weeks hardly anyone went home, except to shower and change. Mukul's shadow haunted every cabin, every desk, every discussion.

Each of the specialists he had hand-picked was fiercely opinionated, and fought to get an idea across. A lesser man would have despaired. Mukul seemed to thrive on this welter of seemingly irreconcilable propositions. He could mesh all their efforts, and channel them in one clear direction. Everyone agreed the resultant synergy was a winner, even when it was contrary to their original perceptions. Some dubbed it malicious cunning. The more charitable called it professional competence. To Mukul, it did not seem to matter. It was as though he had lived all his life for this one great break.

Working almost non-stop, the final presentation slowly began to take a hazy shape. Backgrounders, forecasts, opinion-studies, followed by visuals, the copy, jingles, models, videos, layouts, the media-plan, the cairman's remarks at the pre-launch press conference, and even answers to possible questions – nothing was glossed over. And then as each was honed to perfection, they interlocked like a mysterious jigsaw puzzle. And at the hub of it sat

Mukul, 'like a cruel spider gloating over its prey,' one wisecracked.

Mukul was always dissatisfied, always wanting things to be re-done, and then done all over again. Even a dozen alternatives to pick from did not satisfy him. And with each passing day, he only became more demanding, more exacting. 'A blood-sucker,' they cursed, and yet amazed at what Mukul was drawing out of them, each became increasingly willing, even eager to put in more hours on the job. His obsession seemed to enthral the whole team.

At eleven that morning, the formidable, client team trooped into their conference hall, each carrying bulging folders. From their cynical banter, it was clear that they had been sated by presentations.

Mukul was relaxed, and appeared businesslike. He seated them comfortably, and introduced his chairman and each member of his team. Slipping out of his jacket and folding up his shirtsleeves, he started the presentation. Everyone was amazed at his unflappable calm and quiet confidence. It was not the hard-sell approach. He orchestrated the entire presentation with a low-profile perfection that bordered on wizardry. Each team member was called to step up and do his bit at just the right moment, and waved aside the moment it was over.

None, and this included the client team, realised it had taken almost two hours before he finished. And it was only then that Mukul signalled for cookies and coffee. There had been no interruption. That was step one of the battle won.

The client team went into a huddle, and then the CEO checked his notes, and said the concept was okay, but he wanted the model changed. Someone more 'ethnic', he demanded.

Mukul excused himself, went to his cabin and was back in a few minutes with two sets of cassettes and albums. And to the astonishment of his team and the chairman, he projected both the stills and the song-and-dance sequences by two different models. They had been shot in another studio. He handed over the albums to the CEO who immediately picked one of them. That sewed it up. In less than half-an-hour, the draft MoU Mukul had kept ready was touched up a bit and initialled.

The chairman drove off to his club with the client team for lunch. Mukul stayed back shook hands with each of his colleagues, and asked them to take the rest of the day off.

'Go anywhere you want, do anything you would like to... It's on the house,' he said. 'But be back early tomorrow. There is going to be no let-up on this job.'

He then drove off to join the Chairman for lunch at the club. Over cocktails, the details of the contract were ironed out. The chairman came over and hugged him. The Agency would jump over twenty slots with this account in their bag.

Mukul jerked his car out of the parking lot and squealed out of the hotel gate. The job was done.

'He must have been heading for the children's home for sure,' his secretary sobbed, when she spoke to Salina. 'Even on the busiest day, he would call the matron, to make sure that the kids were okay.' Tears trickled down her face.

'Nice of you to care so much.' Salina consoled the stricken girl.

'What remarkable self-composure,' she later told her colleagues. 'You'd think we had lost more than her. What an ideal match for the GM.'

An ideal match. Behind every successful man. Just for each other. It had begun from their wedding day. At most functions, at every party, someone tossed one of these clichés at them.

She could understand. They were an ideal match. A little over six, wide-shouldered, his stomach flattened by hours of diligent workouts in the gym, Mukul stood out in any group. His long black hair was brushed back with a hint of parting in the centre. The sharp nose over full lips, and a bony chin that jutted gave him a Greek god profile. However, his eyes were close-set and narrow, and this accounted for the tinted glasses he normally wore. He was fastidious about his clothes, and could give any male model a run for his money.

Salina was slender and willowy. Her height underplayed her full-bosomed, well-shaped body, and made her look delicate, even though, once an athlete, she was quite healthy. Her fine-boned face with large wide-set eyes and thick silken hair, loosely knotted at the nape of her neck, enhanced her grace. Her lips were well arched and full without being sensuous. She wore no make-up, and this only added to her good looks.

Mukul, the fast-track executive. Salina, the hostess *par excellence,* with a house admired for its simple elegance, without a touch of ostentation. An ideal match indeed!

In many other ways, they were quite different. Mukul talked a dime a dozen, and his prodigious memory for jokes made him the life of every party. Salina spoke very little even to her close friends. But being a good listener, she always seemed fully involved.

'Why should she strain her vocal chords?' Mukul quipped. 'I'm here to play lead, base and drums for the two of us, plus...'

This made them seem even more complete.

It was, therefore, strange that Salina and Saroja were often found chatting. Saroja, of course, did most of the talking. In the special room booked at the hospital, Salina sat on a comfortable low-slung chair specially provided for her. Saroja squatted on the floor. Salina's soft voice had already influenced Saroja, and she no more spoke loudly in the hospital.

Salina's mind was closed to others. Saroja was extrovert, completely uninhibited, even on what was personal and intimate. Inevitably, she got round to speak of the day of the accident, and once triggered, there was no stopping her.

Vasu had come home late the previous night, she began, and he was drunk. 'I put his food on the oven for warming, after leaving two buckets of hot water in the bathroom. But no Amma, he seemed to have gone mad. He grabbed my arm, but I shook him off, scolding him for coming home drunk. But this made him only more wild and shameless. Oh Amma, how can I tell you this? He dragged me to the back of the house and almost ripped off my *sari* and blouse, his body burning with desire. I lost count of time. There was just him and me, a oneness I had never known before. In a sudden moment of lucidity, I remembered the food on the oven, and holding my *sari* against my bare body, ran to the kitchen. To my horror, it was completely charred. Oh Amma, pardon me for saying all this.'

Salina was silent. But it was as though Saroja wanted to relive all her memories. She was talking more to herself than to Salina.

'By the time he bathed and put on a fresh lungi and vest, I also washed and changed. And then he swept me up as though I was a child, and carried me to the van. And he drove, ever so slowly to the *dhabba* my face against his shoulder. He bought hot chilli-chicken curry, *parottas* and two large omelettes. We sat in the van and he wanted me to feed him, as though he was a child, and he made me share every mouthful he ate.'

'You spend too much money,' I scolded.

'Not today, Saro,' he said. 'All the hundreds of miles I drove, I had only you, your lovely body burning in my mind. The roads, they are very bad at night, Saro,' he said. 'All kinds of girls, even children wave to you. And lorry drivers leave their vehicles on the roadside and disappear with them into hutments, or even behind the bushes. And when they come back, they doze in their seats, allowing the cleaners to have their turn.'

'They laugh at me because I don't go, and sometimes say I'm impotent or even a eunuch. But I can think only of you and your…' 'Oh no Amma, I can't say all this to you. But he said, if ever you touch another man, I will twist his neck and yours like a wet towel. He is so strong, and he will surely do it. But he is my man, all mine, and perhaps he knew it was our last night together…'

For a long time, she wept silently, tears rolling down her cheeks.

'When we got back, he held me close as we walked to our hut, and laid me gently on the bed. Kneeling beside me, he tenderly touched my neck and back, bruised on the ground earlier. And then he got into bed and he was so gentle, asking me every now and then, if he had hurt me. But I could feel my body flare with desire, and I clutched his hair and bit his ear lobe. And then he was a wild animal, livid, brutal. It was as though he could not have enough of me. Nor me of him. How will I ever live without him, Amma? How can I ever forget him? Has he any hope? Will he ever be mine again, Amma?'

Salina remained silent, and her face was blank, except that a muscle in her cheek twitched once or twice. She had sunk deeper into herself. Saroja seemed to have fallen into the trance of her memories, till she felt Salina's hand on her shoulder.

'He will live,' Salina said, and repeated, 'He will live.'

Saroja jerked up, and fell on her knees before Salina. She took her *mangal sutra*, strung on a faded yellow thread around her neck, and pressed it on both her eyelids with reverence.

'May your words come true, Amma.' She was weeping once more, 'May your divine words come true. I want him back. Oh, how I want him back, Amma.'

Early next morning, the chairman said the doctor wanted to speak to her, When they entered the doctor's room, they found him and three of his colleagues, discussing x-rays and cat-scan pictures stuck into the large viewer on the wall. The table was littered with reports.

'Salina,' the chairman began hesitantly. 'For the first time this morning, Mukul had convulsions...'

Salina had guessed something was wrong, and yet she was not ready for this. She seemed to sink a bit deeper in her seat, and her grip on the arms of the chair tightened. The chairman rose and stood beside her, as the doctor spoke.

'There is some fluid accumulation in his skull, and we may have to tap it to prevent both the danger of brain damage, and further convulsions.' His eyes were averted.

'They want your consent for this surgical intervention,' the chairman said, his hand on her shoulder.

'This is a routine...' The doctor began. But Salina stopped him.

'When?' she asked.

'If there are no further convulsions, five tomorrow morning. If not, tonight itself.'

Salina looked up at the chairman for a moment, then picked up the pen, and signed the consent form before her.

'I'll stay over,' she said as she stood up.

'I've already asked the ayah to pack what you may need and come here.' The chairman said. 'I'll send the driver right away..."

'Not her...just the things.' said Salina. Before she left the room, she turned and added almost in a whisper, 'Thanks for your thoughtfulness.'

Back in her room, she sat near the window sipping a glass of water. Saroja's words echoed in her mind. 'I want him back. Oh, how I want him back, Amma.'

No, she couldn't deny it any more. She had encouraged, in fact provoked Saroja to talk about herself. She wanted a shameless peep into another woman's life, to escape from the reality of hers. She knew she could not do that any longer.

Salina's parents had divorced when she, and her only brother, were not even in their teens. Her mother had migrated to the US with her young paramour, taking her son with her. She had never seen or heard from her since. Salina's father was forced to put her in an elite school in a lovely hill resort. He visited her regularly, always with presents, fruits and chocolates. Vacations were spent in their sprawling bungalow, which she inherited with all he owned, when he died of a sudden cardiac arrest. It was Mukul she turned to, for some stability in a life of endless uncertainties.

They had met when he had come over with his chairman for a party her father hosted on one of her vacations. He had just joined the Agency as an Account Executive, after his MBA.

'He is one of the smart ones I was able to pick up during this year's campus recruitment,' his chairman told Salina's father. They were long-time friends, and Salina had known him from infancy.

'He is the only child of his parents, who died together in an air crash. He seems to have all that I'm looking for, to give the Agency a new impetus without which we have no future.'

Mukul was dressed casually that evening. But Salina clearly saw that he was anything but casual in all he said and did. He declined a drink, listening intently to what they spoke, helping them get additional drinks and passing the short-eats. She could see his narrow eyes flash with interest when they talked of the stock market.

It was when dinner was served, that he came over to her.

Nibbling at a leg of chicken, he asked her about her life in finishing school.

'It is the best you can expect from an expensive prison camp,' she said and he couldn't help laughing.

'Are you always so direct?' he asked.

'Direct? I was just telling you the truth.' Salina replied, 'What else did you expect?'

'Girls always make things look a whole lot worse or better,' he quipped, with a wry smile.

'You seem to know a lot about girls,' she countered.

'Now, what is all this?' Her father joined them.

'We were talking about her school, and she said what else can you expect from an expensive prison camp,' Mukul repeated, laughing again.

It was as though the moment suddenly froze. Salina's father almost slumped into a chair, his face ashen.

'Are you all right, Sir?' Mukul asked anxiously.

Salina rose and put her hand on her father's shoulder. 'I was just kidding, Papa,' she said. But Mukul saw her face was a blank mask, even though she seemingly spoke in jest.

He was with Salina's father and his chairman when she passed out. She had invited him, and when he asked his chairman for leave, he said of course, and they could drive over together. Salina's father would also be joining them.

In a white silk *sari,* hand-embroidered in gold *zari,* she came running to the car to receive them. His chairman stooped to kiss her cheek. 'Lovely lady,' he said, and she flushed. Mukul could not take his eyes off her. She was so beautiful.

Soon, the two old friends ambled off to find comfortable seats in the auditorium, leaving Salina and Mukul together. She introduced him to her friends, and did not miss the obvious approval in their eyes. She then left to join the choir, in which she was a lead singer. When the convocation was over, the four of them drove to the restaurant where a table had already been reserved for them. Mellowed by Scotch and an excellent dinner, his chairman stood up to propose a toast.

'I shouldn't really be saying this here, but the setting seems just right. Irresistible!' he began. And then looking directly at Salina, he said, 'The Agency is planning to send Mukul abroad for training.'

'Oh thanks, Sir…' Mukul was clearly caught off-guard.

His chairman sat down, and took a long time lighting his cigar. 'Audio-visual communication is going to bring about a sea change on the media scene, and we don't want to be caught napping, do we, Mukul?' he asked pointedly.

'I've been working on a note on this for you, Sir,' Mukul spoke a bit hesitantly.

'Good,' his Chairman said, puffing deeply at his cigar, and repeated, 'Good.'

Salina put her hand on her father's arm. 'And Sir,' she mimicked 'Are you planning to send me anywhere? And no, I have not yet prepared a note for you, Sir.' The chairman and Mukul laughed.

'You've finished from here in style, darling,' her father said, putting his arm around her. 'But quite honestly, I've no plans for you. I've yet to learn such tricks from this chap.' He pointed his cigarette accusingly at his friend.

'Some plans make themselves,' the chairman said, looking intently at the glowing end of his cigar. He blew out a lung full of smoke, and said, 'And now anyone for a swig of brandy?'

'Not me, Sir.' Mukul said.

'Let us get out of here,' Salina stood up. 'Uncle is polluting the whole of civilisation with wicked cigar smoke.' She kissed him lightly on his head, and Mukul joined her when she left the room.

They did not hear the chairman say, 'They make a marvellous couple.' Salina's father kept staring at them, but said nothing. His silence was loud enough for his friend.

It was cold outside, and Salina shivered, She had not picked up her wrap, draped on the back of her chair in the dining room. Mukul slid out of his jacket and held it, while she slipped in.

'Warm as a cocoon,' she smiled.

Mukul looked directly at her. 'If I go, will you come with me?' he asked.

'Yes,' she said without hesitation.

Their wedding was the social event of the year, and everyone of any consequence was present. They did make a marvellous couple, and the just-for-each-other label stuck from that day.

But now, sitting alone in her room in the hospital, Salina remembered only one thing about the wedding. Mukul had not said he loved her. Nor had she.

She felt an aching loneliness. She called the desk and asked for the special nurse. When she came on the line she wanted her to know if Saroja was around.

'She was here earlier, Madam.' The nurse said. 'But they told her the driver would be out of intensive care tomorrow, and she rushed away to inform her people.'

'Is he well enough to be shifted?' Salina asked.

'Fully conscious. Able to speak clearly and sit up in bed. They have already removed most of the bandages. He will now be shifted to the general ward for treatment of external injuries.'

'Thanks,' and Salina hung up.

She was there, when they wheeled Mukul into the theatre at five the next morning. The chairman had also reached, and when she leaned on him, he put his arm around her. They didn't speak a word.

When Mukul was back in intensive care, the doctors said at the moment things seemed under control. Only another head-scan, and the lab test report of the fluid drawn, would give the correct picture. Till then, they could say and do nothing. Mukul was still unconscious. Salina decided to go home. The routine of the hospital had become choking.

When Salina drove into the portico, her mind went back to the day Mukul had finally agreed to shift to the bungalow. He had picked her up like a doll, and carried her across the threshold. He was so strong. It was this part of their second honeymoon, she always remembered vividly.

Mukul made the most sensuous demands on her. There was no knowing when his desire would flare – on the terrace in a lounge chair, in the cramped seat of the car when they got back home late one night, and even in the bathroom when she showered.

Her quiet upbringing, and the influence of the prim finishing school, had inhibited her passion, to the privacy of their bedroom at night. She knew little about sex, and though she found Mukul irresistible, she was confused, and at times upset by his erotic overtures, He seemed to find endless stimulation in fondling her toes.

Though it was novel and exciting in the beginning, Salina found it difficult to cope with his increasing craving for what she considered unnatural, even abnormal. But she was so completely enthralled by him, that she just let him have his way. He neither drank nor smoked, and was almost paranoid about his personal cleanliness. This seemed compensation enough for what she found irksome.

As she went around the house now, patting a cushion into shape, pushing a book back in place, re-positioning an ashtray with a deft touch, she remembered the day she drove to consult her doctor secretly. Mukul had left for the office. After the routine check-up and tests, the lady doctor, gave her a warm hug, and kissed her on both cheeks.

'And what are you going to call…'

Salina shrieked with joy, and fell into the elderly lady's arms, sobbing with happiness.

'Are you sure?' She asked, her faced hidden in the folds of the doctor's *sari*,

'Well, why don't you wait for a couple of weeks so that you can be sure?' the doctor suggested. When Salina next called, she examined her carefully and said, 'Yes, the baby is on the way.'

'Aunty…Doctor, I'm so...'

'Everything seems to be fine. Just don't do anything silly. Be a bit careful.'

As Salina drove back, she could think of nothing but how to tell Mukul. It was 12.30 in the noon, and Mukul may or may not come home for lunch. He normally called to tell her, or his secretary would inform her. Should she ask him to come? Or, wait till he got back in the evening? Should she tell him over tea, or wait till they were in bed that night? He would surely be more tender and far more considerate, once he knew.

By the time she got home she was so worked up, she could wait no longer. She had to see him immediately. When she reached the office, his secretary said Mukul had left about half an hour ago.

'Was he going home?' She asked, her excitement reaching feverish pitch.

'Yes. Or, else he would have told me,' his secretary said. As Salina was about to leave the room, she added, 'Madam, it is just possible he could have stopped awhile at the Home.'

That was it. Salina drove recklessly to the Home For Handicapped Children. Mukul spent so much time, had collected so much money for this project, and visited it often. He was always so concerned about the children. The watchman saluted, and promptly opened the gate for her.

'The boss went up,' he said, and pointed to the staircase.

Salina took two steps at a time, and burst into the matron's office. There was no one there. The classrooms were also empty, and the playroom too. She came back to the watchman.

'He is not there. No one is around,' she said.

'I'm sure he went up, Madam,' he reaffirmed. Salina saw he was starting his lunch, and realised it was lunch hour, and that the rest of the staff would be in the canteen on the first floor. On her way, she found the door of the dormitory slightly ajar, and not wanting to disturb the children, pushed it slightly open and peeped in.

There were about a dozen children in the room, playing with toys scattered all over the floor. She was surprised to see that all of them were naked. And then she saw Mukul. He was on his knees. He had his back to her, and wore nothing. The matron stood facing her, but her face was tilted upwards, her eyes half-closed. Her blouse was open and her flabby breasts hung out like heavy, shapeless bags. She was holding up a child on a stool, with her arms tight around its chest, and swayed in a frenetic trance, groaning as she kept rubbing her enormous breasts against the back of the child. Mukul, who was crouching, gripped both the knees of the child and his face was buried in its crotch.

Salina froze with shock. But what she saw vividly and would never forget was the child's foolish face, drooling with a promiscuous pleasure it did not understand, and perhaps never would.

Salina spun round, and as she turned, the heel of one slipper caught on the rug and the strap ripped off. She ran down the corridor, and turned into the stairs. Her barefoot slipped on one of the steps, and she found herself tumbling, the floor hurtling towards her.

When she came to senses, she was on the couch in the doctor's clinic, and she was aching all over. The doctor was bent over her, and Salina saw the concern on her face. She writhed with an excruciating stab of pain in her abdomen. Mukul was not there.

'Salina, my dear, I've been so worried,' the doctor said. 'Mukul rushed you here. He couldn't bear to see you like this, and has just gone out. He should be back anytime now.'

As her mind slowly cleared, panic gripped Salina. 'My baby… My baby…' she screamed.

The doctor was silent for some time. 'Now, don't worry too much Salina,' she said in an unsteady voice. 'It is just a miscarriage. Not much damage otherwise. You could have broken your neck falling down those stairs.'

And then, it all came back to Salina, and she began to retch violently, as though she wanted to throw up everything within her, The nurses held her down, and she felt the prick of an injection needle. A warm drowsiness crept over her, and mercifully she dozed off.

It was the chairman who drove her home three days later. When he left, Salina went to the guest room. She never shared a bed with Mukul from that day. And they had been married hardly a year.

It was late in the evening when the telephone rang. The chairman was on the line, 'Have you had anything to eat?' He asked. 'I'm sending the car for you. Come as soon as you can.'

At the hospital, she found Mukul's colleagues in the verandah. They moved to a side, as the chairman led her into the doctor's room. She did not follow what he said. But she understood it was now only a question of time. They let her into the intensive care ward, and she stood looking at Mukul. The special nurse held her hand. The chairman watched with misted eyes through the open door. Her mind was blank. The nurse and the chairman led her out, and went with her to her room in the hospital. She moved like a lifeless puppet.

'Please…' she said, and reluctantly both left.

She was sitting in the chair, her mind still in a daze, when the door was flung open, and Saroja rushed in.

'That woman has been hiding you from me, Amma.' she complained, pointing at the nurse, who had obviously tried to prevent her from entering. 'If she stands in my way again, I will thrash her.' She fell at Salina's feet and burst into tears.

'We are leaving early tomorrow, Amma.' She sobbed. 'They told me you kept Vasu in the hospital. You paid. Oh Amma, why should you suffer so much? I have offered a special prayer at our temple for master and you.'

Salina rang the bell, and the special nurse led Saroja out of the room. Salina knew she would not see her again.

But what she did not know, was that in the tonga the hearse overtook, when they drove Mukul's body to the bungalow the next morning, Vasu lay with his head on Saroja's lap. She ran her fingers through his hair. They were going home.

No More The Same

Pichai sneaked out of the gate, hugging the plastic bags stuffed clumsily under his shirt. He was breathing heavily when he reached his wife, a shadow in the dimly-lit side road. Crouching deeper in the darkness, both stood still, anxiously watching the road. They were alone. Pichai swiftly arranged the bags into the small gunny sack she held open, evened them out, and deftly laced its mouth with a string. When they moved, after she re-draped her *sari*, she seemed heavy with child.

He avoided the terminus, and they boarded the bus from the outer road. The streetlights and garish neon signs streaked past, and the headlight beams soon stabbed the dark highway. Pichai ran a furtive hand over Angamma's belly. The sack was safe. Her discomfort did not bother him.

He stretched in his seat, soaking in the relief that flowed through him. They had escaped. None knew from where they came, or where they were going. Strangely, he did not think of the money. He had just one thought. Life would no more be the same.

*

Vinod slunk to the gate, and scanned the road. The fellow had vanished. He waited – five, ten, fifteen minutes, and went back to the side-room and picked up the duffel bag. Opening the car, he placed it on the floor under the driver's seat and got in. Tension clawed at his throat.

When he drew up, the shop was dark, shuttered. A side-door suddenly opened and snapped shut behind him. He went up the narrow stairs carrying the bag. When he was back, he put the bulging bag in the dicky, and locked it before slipping behind the wheel. He took time sliding the key in the switch, checking if anyone was watching. Reassured, he drove with studied casualness. He had pulled it off. The name and address he had given were false.

The cool breeze was bracing. He smothered the expectations that threatened to storm his mind. One thought persisted – life would now be different.

*

Praveen Sait sat still till he heard the car pull away. He then bolted the door, took the dirty pouches from under his desk and gingerly untied them. He carefully poured the tiny gold beads from each into three large trays. Against the crimson velvet lining, the glistening piles were stunning. He gloated over them. They weighed over 10 kgs, but he had tinkered the scales to show under 8 kgs. And he had sliced the price to sixty per cent of the market rate.

He scooped a palmful of beads, and let them run though his fingers. The feel was exhilarating. He had won on all counts. Smelted in his workshop, its past would be wiped out. And yet after he carefully repacked them into three clean cloth bags, and stowed them in the underground safe, there was only one thought in his mind. So much would now change.

*

Pichai helped Angamma out of the bus at the terminus. They caught another, and reached their village well past midnight. Choosing bylanes, they stole unseen into their hut. The rusty hinges screeched when he pushed the door open. Angamma was groping for the kerosene lamp, when Pichai spun her round and almost ripped off her *sari*, He grabbed the sack, now soaked in sweat, and tore it open in a frenzy. Thrusting his hand in, he punched a hole in one of the plastic bags, and plucked out a bundle of crisp currency notes.

'Mine,' he croaked in a thick guttural voice. 'So much, and all mine.'

Angamma turned away in disgust, re-draping her *sari*, as Pichai climbed a wooden stool and craftily concealed the sack behind the firewood and cow-dung cakes piled in the loft. Dismounting, he threw himself on her, wrestling her down to the bare unswept floor. He was grunting with lust.

'Shame on you,' she snapped, as she tried to roll away. 'I haven't even washed.'

'Afterwards, afterwards,' he growled, clawing away her clothes. She struggled, but he pinned her down. The sweat stink of his unwashed body nauseated her. When she finally managed to roll away from him, he was already snoring, his mouth open.

She pulled off her *sari* and flung it on the floor. There was a little water in the mud pot. Carrying it outside, she washed, scrubbing hard, as though this would absolve her of what she was forced to do in the past few days. In a clean, though crumpled, blouse and skirt, her long wavy hair trailing in the breeze, she sat in the dark verandah, sick at the thought of even being in the same room with Pichai.

*

Vinod thrust the duffel bag into Usha's hands as soon as he reached home. 'Lock it up,' he said, as he breezed into the bathroom. Usha heard the shower gush, and smiled as he shouted for a towel. He had forgotten, as usual.

In clean white kurta-pyjamas, he poured himself a drink, and dropped into his favourite wicker chair in the sit-out of their bedroom, his feet propped on the railing. He soaked in the safety of the silent night. Draining the glass quickly, he poured himself another and sauntered back, swirling the ice cubes in the tumbler.

When he got into bed, Usha was asleep. Gently snapping open the buttons of her flimsy slip-on, he traced the curve of her small firm breasts and slid his hands down the warm satin-smoothness of her waist and hips. Strangely, it did not arouse him. He slithered downwards clumsily, trying to get his lips to her nipples, but she grumbled in sleepy protest and turned away. He waited for the usual surge of passion. In vain.

What had happened? Had he drunk too much? Or, was he drained by the day's pressures? He got out of the bed and poured himself another drink. A stiff one. He would get back to bed after finishing it.

The next morning, Usha woke him from his chair in the sit-out. He was aching all over, and his head was splitting. He gulped the aspirins with the black coffee she gave him, and as soon as she tucked him into bed, he was fast asleep.

*

Praveen Sait reached home well past ten. He wheeled his scooter into the portico and locked the gate. To his surprise, Anila opened the door for him. His parents had long gone to bed. After he showered, she helped him dry his hair, holding his face against her soft belly. The food she served was hot, delicious, and the pan, sweet and scented.

As usual, he went about checking the doors. When he got into bed, Anila turned towards him, and her lips were wet, craving, her breasts taut with desire. She wore nothing.

Over and over again, she aroused him, and it was as though the magic of that night would never end. Finally, when they fell apart, she snuggled close to him. He dropped off to sleep, aware for the first time that Anila was no more the coy, submissive girl he had married eighteen months ago.

*

Pichai did not go to work for Narayana Achari after they returned. He told him the doctor in the city had asked him to rest and take medicines, and not to carry weights for some time. The kindly old man was concerned. Pichai was one of his best stone-carvers, always entrusted with intricate finishing work.

'Take rest,' he said. 'Get well soon. You have yet to complete the Bhagavathy idol for the new temple on the hillock.'

Pichai stumbled home drunk every night. Pretending to go to the toilet, he would often sneak out, and swig from a bottle he had hidden in the bushes. And then he would awkwardly wolf his food, falling asleep at times without even washing his hands. Angamma did not care, because she was sick of his breath reeking of cheap liquor, and his filthy body-smell. He was repulsive in bed, tumbling over her in drunken stupor, often exhausting himself even as he tugged at her clothes.

She had hated him from the beginning. Her father, also a shameless drunkard, had been a master stone-carver working for Narayana Achari. In a few weeks of her mother's death during her second childbirth, he married a girl more than twenty years younger than him. It was Pichai who often helped him home when he was sloshed.

The day Pichai carried her father home and dumped him on the mat was etched in her mind. He had puked all over Pichai's clothes, and after bathing at the well he came in, wearing a clean lungi her stepmother gave him. She ogled his bare body when she served food. Angamma went to sleep in the kitchen. Her father sprawled in drunken stupor on the mat.

A loud strangled cough woke her, and when she ran into the main room, her father was struggling to sit up. He was vomiting and clutched at his throat. Her stepmother was not with him.

She rushed out calling for her, thinking she had gone to the toilet. She heard a strange rasping behind the well, and peeped. Her stepmother lay naked on the ground, her arms tight around Pichai. Her legs were entwined around his haunches, and his muscles tensed as he pounded her on the ground, till with a strangled cry, she tore his hair with her hands pleading with him to stop. Suddenly, he slumped, and she whimpered as she clung to him. With the soles of her feet, she stroked the back of his thighs.

Angamma fled back to the hut shouting, but by the time both reached, her father had choked on his vomit. When Pichai pulled him up, his head flopped back. He was dead.

Like most women in the locality, her stepmother soon took to bootlegging, and starting coming home tipsy. And then the police raided their hut, and took her away. Pichai came that evening and said he would have to stay, as Angamma was not safe alone. The police may come again. He repeatedly raped her that night. Bruised, disgraced, with nowhere to go, she began cooking for him the next day. Her stepmother did not come back.

*

Vinod never admitted it. He may not even have been aware, that almost everything he did or didn't, was in revolt against his father.

He was the only child of the elderly pastor, who lost his vivacious wife during Vinod's birth. He remained single, retreating deeper into religion, and a life of total self-denial. To him, it was pleasure that took his wife, and so all enjoyment was a sin.

Vinod started smoking before he passed school, and could tipple half a bottle of rum when he was in the engineering college. He worked out for hours at the gym, and read everything that came his way, except the Bible.

Exceptionally intelligent and hard-working, he majored with honours in Medico-Engineering. On a merit scholarship, he joined a business school, and was voted the first in his class likely to make a million.

Vinod had spotted Usha even in school. She was the girl who came in a spanking white Mercedes Benz, which returned to pick her in the evening. In the noon, her ayah brought lunch, and as he munched soggy sandwiches, he watched her lay out casseroles of hot food on a picnic rug under a shady tree. The napkins were sparkling white and often there was ice cream.

Usha was one of the cheerleaders when he played soccer for his school team. And he was in the front seat when she sang lead for the choir. Otherwise, it remained a hi-hi friendship. She kept in touch with him when he went to the management school. It was after he was selected by a leading multinational for advanced training abroad, that he picked up the confidence to ask her if she would marry him when he came back to take over as General Manager (Product Development). 'I cannot think of life without you,' he told her.

Her soft-brown eyes fixed on him, she took a long time to reply.

'Yes, Vinod. But only if your father agrees,' she said.

When he asked his father, he said nothing.

'But you will surely attend the wedding?' Vinod stuttered. He always seemed to stammer when he spoke to his dad.

The old man closed his eyes and nodded. 'But I will live separately, he said.

Vinod married Usha according to a Hindu ceremony. They moved into the posh flat his company had provided him, elegantly furnished by Usha's father. The day they moved in, Vinod carried his drink to the wicker chair in the sit-out of their bedroom, and propped his legs on the railing. He had achieved his first goal in life on the double.

There was little they lacked, and if there were no children immediately, it was because they had planned it that way. Though it was never called a dowry, Usha's father had invested an enormous sum in shares in her name, but managed it himself, with a consummate skill that amazed Vinod.

He bought a computer, fed into it the best stock market software available, and spent late nights keying in an imaginary portfolio for himself.

'Out of your Dad's shadow into my father's?' Usha teased.

'Just you wait till I get started.' He laughed. Usha talked to him about 'borrowing' money from her dad, but Vinod turned it down flat.

'I will do it on my own,' he said,

'Still under your Dad's spell?' She rubbed her nose on his shoulder.

'Now, under yours,' he replied, as he picked her up and carried her to bed.

*

Praveen was the last of nine children. Everyone said he was born lucky. As each of his elder brothers and sisters married, they moved out, Praveen would inherit the house and his father's pawnshop, according to community and family tradition.

On completing school, his father asked if he would like to join college, or start working in his pawnshop. Praveen consulted his mother, whose guidance he always sought.

'Take possession of the shop soonest possible,' she advised. 'One never knows what can happen.' He joined his father. By twenty, he had learned the intricacies of money lending. In his twenty-first year, his mother found him a beautiful slender bride. Being the last wedding in the family, his father made it memorable, with greater pomp and pageantry than in all the previous weddings in the family. Anila and he stayed with his parents.

Anila's brother had long ago started a business in Singapore, and when he was back on vacation or work, he teased Praveen for limiting himself to what he scoffed as 'petty money lending'. 'Yes, you have a comfortable existence. But what else? Everyday – the same dry routine. Soon, your mind will be set in a die – lending, recovering and writing up ledgers.'

'What else can I do?' Praveen asked. 'You must remember I joined father after school.'

'Money is shifting to real estate. To stocks and shares. And you can make a hundred times more.'

When they were alone in the shop one day, Praveen asked his father. The old man was silent, and Praveen began to wonder if he had heard him. After they had finished dinner that night, and the ladies had left to wash the dishes, he cleared his throat.

'About dealing in land and shares,' he began. 'What do you know about this business?'

'Nothing,' Praveen admitted. 'But Anila's brother knows, and says he will guide me.'

'And who will invest?' his father asked.

'He is prepared to invest fifty per cent. He says we can get low-interest loans from banks up to four times our investment.'

'First go and consult the astrologer. Tell me what he has to say, and then we can talk further.' The astrologer said Praveen's horoscope showed bright prospects for a new business. He even forecast a windfall.

'Limit both your buying price, and the prices at which you will sell. Never expect too much. That is not business. It is speculation. Gambling. There is no tradition of gambling in our family, and there should never be.' His father made it clear.

Praveen started, began to prosper, and shifted his new business to a room alongside his father's office.

Everything seemed to go right, except that they had no children even after eighteen months of marriage. But this did not irk him so much as the strict financial limits his father set for his new business. He wanted more money.

*

Pichai told Angamma, Narayana Achari wanted to see her.

'I have chosen you for a very sacred task,' he began. He was a giant of a man, with a shock of white hair, his forehead always smeared with *vibhuti.* He was deeply religious and observed all sorts of vows. Often, he fasted, weeks at a time.

The hillock on the outskirts of the nearby town had been bought by a wealthy contractor to build a new hotel, he told her. But when he started construction, something stalled the work. He consulted his guru. From an elaborate astrological ritual, it emerged that there was once a temple on the hillock, now in ruins swamped by undergrowth. The gods were angry, and would not allow any work, till a

Durga temple was built and consecrated there. Narayana Achari was the *shilpi* chosen for this shrine.

'The exact plot has been marked, Angamma. I want you to help clear the site. You must bathe daily before you start work. Always knot your hair above your head. Never let it fall loose when you are working there. This is important. Be a strict vegetarian, and Pichai, you keep away from her. I will pay her twice the normal wage.'

Angamma revered the old man. Early next morning, she bathed, prayed at the wayside Devi temple, and started the work. It soon entranced her, and she could work for hours without tiring. The plot was cleared quickly. Narayana Achari came, and he was pleased. He stood still for a long time, his eyes closed.

'Only you could have done this, Angamma. You are blessed.' he said, and added. 'And now you must also help excavate the foundation after I demarcate it. I will depute three others to help you. You must not give up your vow of purity.'

The sun beat down mercilessly. The ground was crusty. Others shirked work by midday. But nothing held back Angamma.

They were soon down about four feet, and often in the noons Angamma worked alone. One day, her pickaxe ricocheted against something and almost grazed her ankle. Angamma's eyes were glued to the ground. A blood-stained gash seemed to emerge from the ground.

She carefully dug around it with her bare hands. She did not notice that in the blazing sky a cloud had formed, casting a shadow over the site. It became unbelievably cool.

It was an old copper urn, so heavy she could not lift it. She quickly covered it with bramble and hastened out of the pit to inform Narayana Achari. But Pichai was coming towards her. They normally shared the cold rice she brought for their afternoon meal.

'Where are you going?' he asked.

'For some drinking water,' she lied.

'Anything the matter?' he demanded. There was a glow on her face, a radiance. And her breath came in little gasps. He caught her arm and twisted it behind her.

'What have you been up to? Tell me.' And before she could reply, he forced her to the site.

She pleaded in vain, but his hands tightened on her throat and he said he would kill her if she spoke to anyone. He picked up the urn and carried it away. Late that night, he came home with three heavy pouches. Before daybreak, they caught the bus to the city, the flattened pouches in a small sack fastened under Angamma's *sari*. Pichai found a hut abandoned by construction workers, buried the pouches in a corner and placed a large stone on top. It was only then that he took out a small dirty bag tucked into his waist. Untying the string that fastened its mouth, he carefully poured into his hand, a small scoop of gold beads. He laughed when he saw she was surprised. For the first time she realised what had been in the urn. Gold beads. And it belonged to the Devi. A cold shiver went through her and his mocking laugh was like a vice tightening around her heart.

'We must find a buyer,' he said. 'Don't move from here. I will look around. If you try any funny stunts, I will twist your neck and burn you alive in this hut. No one will know or care.'

Angamma knew she was helpless. He had already destroyed her body. Now, he was destroying what was left of her life.

*

Vinod's day began with a brisk jog. In a spanking tracksuit, he ran a carefully chosen route, avoiding both early traffic and dirty roads. As he jogged past the hutments recently abandoned by workers who had finished work on the new multi-storeyed building three streets away from his, he saw a bleary-eyed man squatting in front of one of the crumbling huts. He disliked him at first sight.

After a couple of days, he noticed the chap furtively watching him. Driving home from work, he saw him sneak past his house.

The next day, he ran a little away from the hut and immediately turned back. The rascal was just coming out to peep in the direction he had taken.

'What is your game?' Vinod demanded. 'You want accommodation in jail?'

'*Ayya, Ayya, Ayya,*' the man whined, almost falling at Vinod's feet. 'Please, don't misunderstand me. I have come from my village because my wife is very ill and needs immediate treatment. I thought you may help. *Ayya,* please save her.'

Vinod never fell for sob stories. He jogged away. The next day, he saw the chap standing outside the hut, his hands folded. He glimpsed someone lying still inside.

'What's wrong with her?' he snapped, annoyed at having to pause.

'Cancer,' the man said. 'Very serious.'

'Come to my gate after I get back from work tonight. I will give you a note to the hospital.' And he jogged away.

He was there that evening, servile, more disgusting than ever. Vinod pencilled the name and address of the Cancer Institute and a doctor he knew, on a slip of paper.

'Go there at seven tomorrow morning,' he said.

The man tried to fall at Vinod's feet. 'No need for this drama,' he snapped.

'I have something more to tell you, *Ayya,*' he pleaded. 'Please, let me come in for a few minutes.'

The chap took out the small dirty pouch tucked in his waist, and held it out to Vinod.

'What's this nonsense?' Vinod almost barked.

'Please, see,' the chap entreated. 'Then, we can talk.'

Vinod shuddered at the thought of touching the sweat-stained pouch.

'*Ayya*, please let me come in and show you,' he begged.

Vinod did not know why he let him in. Usha was having a shower when they entered the side-room, and she did not see him. The man swiftly untied the string fastening the pouch, and slid some gold beads into his palm.

'Oh no, I don't want your ornaments. I was just trying to help.' Vinod was furious. He would have hit him, if he did not look so filthy. But the man would not budge. He poured the remaining beads into his palm and stretched it towards him.

Vinod had never been enamoured by gold or any ornaments. He wore nothing other than his thin wedding band. But something prompted him to touch the beads. He could not take his eyes off them.

'What the hell do you want? I am going to hand you over to the police,' he snapped.

'*Ayya*, please. Please, believe me. I found it when I was digging the foundation for a building. You can ask my wife. We have three full bags. You can get it tested anywhere.'

During the next two days, Vinod carefully picked a pawnshop on the other side of the town. He gave a false name and address. The smart young chap there did exhaustive tests, and confirmed it was pure 24-carat gold.

'24 carat, and pure?' Vinod was surprised.

'I guarantee, sir,' he said.

'Will you buy it?' Vinod asked, trying to sound casual.

'Yes,' the man said immediately. 'In cash. As much as you have.'

Vinod took the three pouches from Pichai for further sampling. The tests confirmed its purity. That night, he paid off the fellow who immediately vanished. Later, he kept his appointment with the pawn-walla. He had his nest egg, just when the stock market was looking up!

*

Praveen never had it so good. They had launched into real estate at the right time. A civil engineer he had once befriended, tipped him off about a new highway that would bypass the city, diverting heavy vehicles from its over-clogged roads. It was called the Ring Road. It would also be the city's only link with the new wholesale market being re-sited in the suburbs.

He spoke to his brother-in-law, and they bought large tracts of land adjoining the proposed alignment of the new road. He did not tell his father that he had borrowed heavily to finance this. But the road did come up, and land value alongside shot up by ten, fifteen times. His father looked impressed when he told him this had brought unimaginable returns.

At home, life was even better. Anila was well into her eighth month, and after a scan the doctors hinted it could be a boy, and all was well.

So much money was flowing in, that he hardly remembered the bags of gold beads in his safe. He had not told Anila or his brother-in-law. But when he was alone in the office late nights, he would take them out, and was always thrilled when he let the beads run through his fingers. Almost like fondling Anila's breasts. Sometimes, it even aroused him, and in the night he would be demanding, and Anila, now protected with pillows, still responded with passion.

One day, when they lay still after taking the most out of each other, he asked her what sort of gift she would like when the baby was born.

'Anything from you,' she said.

'More than this?' he asked leaning down, to rub his lips on her breasts. He placed his face gently on her abdomen.

'No,' she said, fondling his face. 'Not more than this.'

But he had decided. A special necklace with fifty pendants of solid 24-carat gold. He had already asked a goldsmith to make the die. If he was satisfied, he himself would melt the beads into bars, before giving him the gold.

The die was perfect, a mystic design. He told Anila he would be late that night, and worked the furnace all by himself, melting the beads into small bars.

When he reached home, Anila did not open the door for him. His mother came down. She said Anila was not feeling well and was in bed.

That night Anila woke up crying. He was scared her pains had started prematurely, but it was a dream that had terrified her. She was almost incoherent. There was this beautiful woman, she mumbled, shining like gold, coming towards her. Suddenly she turned and walked away, and Anila found her stomach flat, as though she had snatched away her baby.

'Silly girl,' he chided as he held her close. 'Did you eat too much tonight?'

'Let her sleep with me a few nights,' his mother said the next morning. 'These things happen. She is more beautiful than ever, and with your business booming, someone must have cast evil eyes on both of you.'

*

Angamma always stopped at the Devi temple on her way to work. Fresh after a bath, she received the *Aarti* and *Prasad* from the priest. On her way back, covered with dust and grime, she just stopped to bow from the road, outside the temple. One day she turned to find Narayana Achari watching her.

'About Pichai…' he began. Angamma stood with downcast eyes and said nothing. 'Why didn't you tell me earlier?' he asked. She remained silent. 'I know my child,' the elderly man continued. 'I know everything. Except where he gets so much money. One thing I want to say. My home is always open for you. My wife loves you like a mother.' Angamma wept silently.

She had long stopped talking to Pichai. He was invariably asleep when she left for work and when she got back, he was never at home.

He no more forced himself on her. But he was increasingly menacing. Slumped in a corner of the room, arms and legs askew, she caught ominous snatches from his slurred words.

'…It's mine now, only mine …she wants it. That bitch… Angamma, she's no good. Useless. I must find another. You come, come if you dare… I'll…'

Sometimes, when he took money from the sack in the loft, some currency notes fluttered to the floor. Angamma tied them to the end of the pallav of her *sari*, and the next day she put it in the temple *hundi*.

'Forgive me Mother,' she prayed.

*

Vinod was by now well known in the stock market. Even experienced players sought his views. None knew he had been working on a whole range of portfolio combinations for well over a year.

Back from work, he would kick off his shoes and sit before his computer, feed in data scribbled on a pocket memo-pad, and then pour over sheaves of printouts. He was familiar with the balance sheets of scores of companies, and read almost all the main financial publications late into the night.

Unknown names had zoomed into the headlines, with stories of sensational bids, takeovers, windfalls.

'How would you like to move into a beach house?' Vinod asked Usha. As usual, her eyes were calm, steady.

'Papa says this is a balloon, Vinod,' she replied. She knew Vinod was treading unchartered ground.

'Your dad was always a pessimist, dear,' he teased.

'You look tired,' she cautioned. 'You sleep too little.'

She did not add he drank too much, hardly ate anything, and had stopped workouts. He had been flogging himself with work. Ever since he came home with that cursed duffel bag, he seemed to be avoiding her, working on his computer into the small hours of the morning and falling asleep the moment he stumbled into bed. And he was always in a hurry.

She spoke to her father, who was deeply concerned when she mentioned a few names Vinod had been dropping. 'Those chaps are not investors. They are manipulators. They are going beyond all limits, and the consequences will be disastrous.'

'But Papa, Vinod seems too deep into this and he refuses to turn round,' she replied.

'Just tell him, I've long stopped both buying and selling,' he said. 'The market is a minefield. Anything can happen.'

When she told Vinod, he laughed. 'Stop? Now? When the moment for the kill has come? One big deal and I'll relax, darling. Just one big deal.'

That day, he asked her for the duffel bag. 'Vinod, are you sure…?'

'Never surer,' he smiled, and leaned down to kiss her. When his car has squealed out of the gate, she dropped into a chair, and burying her face in her hands began sobbing.

*

Praveen could not take his eyes off the necklace. He had seen a lot of gold jewellery. But he had never seen a piece like this. The goldsmith who had made it also seemed entranced by his creation.

'I can't believe I did it. It is a piece for a goddess. Who else can wear this?' he asked in awe.

'It's good,' Praveen admitted. He was always sparing in his praise. It tended to increase the wage bill. But when he asked the goldsmith his making charges, his reply came like a slap on his face.

'I can't take anything for this. I can't. From the moment I started, it was almost as though it made itself. No Saitji, I can't take money for this,' and before Praveen could say anything, he backed off.

Praveen fondled the necklace. Yes, what the man said was true. It was a rare creation, the like of which he had never seen. 'A piece for a goddess,' the chap had said. For a fleeting moment he wondered about the gold beads.

A telephone call from his mother cut into his thoughts. Anila had been admitted to hospital, she said.

*

Pichai lunged at Angamma, missed, and fell on his knees. 'I must kill you. I must kill you. Or, you will take it away. You will tell that swine Narayana Achari. He wants to sleep with you. I'll kill him too,' he muttered.

Angamma had heard these drunken threats. But Pichai was unusually menacing. He grabbed her hair and flung her into a corner of the room and stood swaying before her. He had a bottle of kerosene in his hand, and fumbled for the matchbox in his pocket.

'No, not yet,' he mumbled to himself. 'I must first take the money, before I twist your neck, pour kerosene on you and set fire to this hut.'

He just managed to mount the stool, and grabbed the sack hidden in the loft. It fell on the ground with a thud and burst. The kerosene bottle also crashed and the oil splashed on the bundles of currency notes scattered on the floor with dried cow-dung cakes.

Angamma tried to drag him away, but he lashed out blindly. 'You bitch. You slut. You're trying to take my money.' He lit a matchstick, which snapped, struck another, slipped and fell. A tiny flame licked a bundle of currency notes. Pichai tried to beat out, but it only fanned the flame, and the flicker turned into a blaze, which soon swept the floor.

Angamma fled outside screaming for help. But by the time people came running, the flames, fed by paper, and cow-dung cakes now soaked in kerosene had leapt high, engulfing the room and the thatched roof above. They could barely see Pichai burning like an effigy, clasping a flaming sack to his chest.

Angamma's hair had fallen loose, and her *sari* trailed behind her. Pointing at the raging flames, she suddenly stopped screaming, slapped her thighs and burst into hysteric laughter, her hair thrashing around her face, like one possessed.

It was when Narayana Achari gently put his hand around her shoulders, that she fell silent and looked up. 'Father,' she whispered as she slumped in his arms.

There was little left of the hut by the time the fire engine reached. The charred body they retrieved was a grotesque jumble of burnt stumps.

*

Vinod could not believe it. No. He could not go wrong. No way. He had worked out every possible angle. Talked to those who had sound inside information. Yes, insiders themselves. The stock was bound to soar a minimum of five to ten times, the moment the takeover by the multinational was announced the next day. Even the press conference had been called, and he was invited. Buyers were berserk, buying even tiny lots, at unimaginable prices.

He had thrown everything he had in a massive buyout. Everything including the whole margin the bank had allowed him, all that his friends had generously drummed up, and the entire contents of the duffel bag. Yes, he was the major player this time. He went home tired, deeply contented. He would wake up the next day a millionaire many times over.

But as he lingered over his after dinner cognac, he caught the newsflash in the late night telecast. The government had ordered some arrests. There was talk that the exchange was being closed the next day. He heard the word scam. He called his broker, who was so tense, he could hardly speak.

'I'll get back to you.'

Past eleven, Vinod could not bear the suspense any longer. He had started drinking from the bottle. The broker still kept saying, 'I'll get back to you.'

'I must go and see what is happening,' he growled. Usha tried to stop him from leaving, but he pushed her aside. He was unsteady and stumbled as he ran to the car.

The road in front of the broker's office was jammed by vehicles and a crowd that seemed to have gone crazy. Vinod could not even approach the building.

He drove to the nearest empty phone-booth and called Usha. 'Get your dad on the other line. Quick.' He snapped.

'I'll hold this. No, I'll call him myself. There is no time to waste.'

The old man was slow, very deliberate when he spoke.

'You have a holding in Blue Mont?' He asked in obvious astonishment.

'Yes. Yes. Yes.' Vinod screamed into the mouthpiece.

'Vinod, go home fast. I will come over. We can talk from there.'

'Tell me. Tell me now.' Vinod yelled. There was another pause, and then Usha's father's voice was very low, but clear.

'Blue Mont prices have dropped.' Mercifully, he did not use the word crashed.

When Vinod started the car, he did not even know the direction in which he was driving. He just wanted to get away from the broker's office. As he picked up reckless speed, he realised he was heading away from home. He made an abrupt sweeping U-turn.

The brakes of the truck trailing behind him screeched as the driver desperately tried to swerve away from the car across the road. He failed, and smashed head-on into its side, sending it cart wheeling like a toy, and then ran over it before skidding to a stop. All that was left of the car was an ugly mangled mess of twisted metal.

When Usha's father reached home, he found her slumped in the sit-out. Her face was a lifeless mask and she stared at him as though he was a stranger.

*

Praveen tore into the hospital to find his mother and aunt beaming with excitement in the lobby outside the delivery room.

'Within minutes of reaching here, Anila was taken to the delivery room, and by the time I rushed back here after calling you from the booth, she had delivered,' his mother gushed.

Anila was soon wheeled into the room, followed by a nurse carrying the baby – fair, dark-haired, unbearably beautiful.

'He seemed in a hurry to come,' the nurse smiled, as she placed the baby gently beside Anila.

Praveen's eyes filled. Every dream, every prayer of his seemed to have been answered. As he leaned to kiss the baby on his head, his cheek brushed Anila's breast. He would never forget the deep contentment and pride in her tired face. He sat on the edge of the bed just staring at her. His mother and aunt pattered about whom the baby resembled.

Anila and the baby were back home in two days. Oil-baths, hot-packs and specially prepared food made Anila lovelier than ever. His aunt got a godman to tie a knotted string around her wrist, and she always put a black dot on the baby's cheek to ward off evil eyes.

Praveen had decided to give Anila the necklace at the christening ceremony on the twelfth day. When he showed it to his father, he was startled, and looked at him sharply. He hesitated, before giving it to his wife. Everyone wanted to see and feel it, before his mother put it around Anila's neck carefully arranging the pendants. It glittered as it hung down her chest. Indeed, a piece for a goddess.

'It is so lovely, so solid,' his mother said proudly.

Anila was cradling the baby in her arms and someone looped the long necklace round the baby's neck saying, 'It's for both of them, for both of them.'

There was so much merriment in the room, that no one saw Anila's eyes narrow into slits. Her nostrils flared and she started breathing harshly. Suddenly, she stood up, and the baby slipped from her arms. Praveen's mother screamed pointing at the baby strangling on Anila's breasts as the necklace tightened like a noose around its neck.

Arms dangling Anila fell face-forward, her head hitting the edge of a chair.

Praveen frantically spun her round and struggled to free the baby from the necklace twisted tight round its broken neck. Then holding up its limp lifeless body, he dropped on his knees beside Anila, howling in anguish.

Steep Steps To Nowhere

Vasu couldn't believe it. Was this the girl he married, just because she was so different from every other he had known? Roopa always looked at life with a topsy-turvy squint, making almost everything easy to face, easy to handle. And she was always bubbling with an impish humour few could resist.

He hated to say this, but pressed on, 'You know your condition, Roopa. The doctors have warned that your pelvic fracture could make this a Caesarean. That my age and yours, makes this a precious baby. And yet…yet you want to go to your ancestral home, in that…in that…that far-off village, to have our baby?' He just held back from saying godforsaken place.

'I know you will not understand, Vasu.' Roopa's voice was soft, her face turned towards him. He loved this most about her. She always looked at people with an open face as though she had nothing to hide.

'How can you even think of this, Roopa?' Vasu was aghast. 'It's miles away from a *pucca* hospital. Far out even from a doctor. Yet, you want to go there to have our baby? It's incredible, Roopa.'

'I know how you feel, Vasu. Your concern for our baby …for me…'

'Oh! Roopa, she is our baby. Our very own. We must have her. We must…we must…' he repeated, as though this would change her mind.

'I promise you one thing, Vasu,' Roopa's voice was faint, but clear. 'Our baby will be safer there, than anywhere else.'

It was like chopping off all further talk.

'Please Vasu, let's not go over this again…I'm …I'm…'

Vasu could see she was tired, bone-weary. He did not know his fists were clenched, till he felt Roopa's hands around them. And their softness drained the tension, the fear that petrified him. He leaned his face in the groove of her neck, and the freshness of her hair blotted out everything but his love for her.

And he knew in his heart, he could not change her mind. Roopa was sweetness itself, but nothing could soften, let alone melt the steel in which her faith was cast.

Good God, what a girl he had married.

He had just to think of Roopa, and tenderness washed over him. He had topped both in the engineering college and in his management school. With his boyish looks and abundant energy, jobs were his for the asking during campus recruitment. He chose a small to medium company, because the chairman who talked to him was honest, direct. Yes, they were in bad shape now, he said. But he had faith in his company, in his staff, its products, its future. And would Vasu help him turn it round?

He joined at half the salary the bigger companies offered, and was at full stretch into work. Nothing daunted him. Now, almost ten years later, well into his thirties, he was Chief Executive, and the company, a blue-chip on every stock market. And he was still single. His mother had all but given up persuading him to marry.

'Leave me alone, Mom,' he parried. 'Maybe, I'm not the marrying type. The girl I want has not yet surfaced.'

'What rubbish,' she chided, pretending to be angry. 'I have shown you so many girls. I can't understand what you are looking for, Vasu.'

'Looking for?' And then uncertainly, 'I really don't know, Mom. Maybe, I'm not looking at all.'

'Soon you will be so old, no girl will have you.' She scolded gently, putting her hand on his cheek. 'I'm not growing any younger, Vasu. Once you are married there is nothing…'

'Check,' Vasu chuckled, 'except that you would then want a grandson and a granddaughter, and then…'

'Oh! Vasu. You are so like your father. You hide your deepest feelings by making people laugh. But I know you are lonely, that you need someone. How I wish…'

'That God, in his infinite mercy, will spare a girl the endless agony of life with Vasu,' and he was off to work.

But sometimes, all alone after a tiring day, or an unavoidable party, he could not deny the emptiness ahead. Where was this taking him? The thrill of success had already worn thin. Would this monotony never end?

He would steal into his mother's room, for a glance at her sleeping face. She had given her life for him. His father, a leading lawyer, extrovert, popular had dropped dead in his prime. She was only in her twenties then, and she must have been a very attractive girl. Even now, in her fifties graceful and vivacious, she was a superb hostess, who could turn out a delicious meal in a trice, and smile away the off-colour jokes of his less sensitive friends. For her sake, he should find a girl, to give her the company she craved. But who, where was this girl? What was he looking for?

He had never been carried away by good looks. Ten minutes into a conversation, he ran out of small talk. Except to say something funny, and hear the exaggerated laugh, which he knew was just to please him. And this only added one more cold layer of distrust.

The visit to the school for handicapped children was unexpected. His chairman had donated a new wing to the building, and could not make it to the inauguration.

'Vasu, please go on my behalf,' the old man had telephoned. This must be very special, thought Vasu. The chairman had called him at the office, and again reminded him at home early that morning. As always, Vasu took his mother when he made social calls. He was in an unpleasant mood.

'You cut that blinking tape, Mom, and I hope it will be garish pink. The colour you hate most,' he snapped.

'Oh! Vasu, you remember, everything, even my aversion to pink. The girl who marries you will be really lucky.'

'Oh! there you go again. Where does a girl come into this? Let me get your shawl. It will be cooler when we drive back…' and he came back with the hand-embroidered lime-green wrap, his gift on her last birthday.

Vasu disliked social do-gooders. Uneasy in the chief guest's chair, he wondered why his chairman had given so much money for this huge building. For nothing less than a vital business concession from a minister, a bureaucrat? He knew his chairman well. If he was here, there would be sweet talk of love and service, all that syrupy stuff on which these functions floated. Why couldn't they just get going without this tape-cutting stuff?

He had made sure that his mother was seated comfortably. He glanced at her, and did not miss the pride in her face, seeing him represent his chairman. Row upon row of children in their best clothes squirmed in their seats. Why was he wasting time here? He had brought home the sales manager's report on the new product launch, and wanted to study it for the meeting two days hence.

A gentle voice from behind startled him, 'Will you please come down and give sweets to the children?'

'I think my mother will do that,' he said a bit abruptly.

'Brave lady. But will it be a terrible strain to come down three steps to accompany her?' He turned and saw a girl looking him full in the face. Her eyes were dancing with mischief. To his surprise, she was already leading him down the stage to his mother. 'You'd look great in a Santa outfit,' she whispered impishly.

He saw the delicate curve of her neck, and the gleam of

the single string of pearls she wore. Her thick hair was loosely knotted, but stayed in place. And as he followed her, for no reason he felt club-footed, and tripped on the wires of the sound system. She turned round a moment, and he saw her naughty smile, as though she enjoyed his annoyance.

He went to his mother, and taking her by her arm walked her to the children. 'Mom, save me from this fuss,' he said under his breath, 'That smartie wants to make a fool of me.'

He didn't know why he said that, and he missed his mother's searching glance. But when they reached the children, there she stood, a tray of sweets in her hand. His mother took one and gave it to a child. The little girl reached out eagerly, but just could not get hold of it. Her fingers seemed to move like disjointed clamps.

'Please, hold this,' the girl said quickly to Vasu, pushing the tray into his hands. And kneeling, she took the child's hand in hers, and slowly shaped the tiny fingers to take the sweet from his mother. When she got hold of it, the child gurgled with delight, holding it tight in her grubby fist, and said something he couldn't understand.

'She is thanking you, Mrs Sreenivasan,' the girl said.

'Oh! I'm so sorry… I did not realise…,' his mother stammered. As they went from child to child, the tray still in his hand, he saw the easy grace with which she moved, and the compassion in all she did.

Unexpectedly, she slipped back and asked cheekily, 'Will it be too much strain to give one sweet?' His mother laughed at his embarrassment. And again, when the girl said, 'It is for your mother. And you too can have one. But only if you first put a toffee in your mother's mouth.'

And he was again looking at that impish face turned towards him, and saw the laughter in her eyes as she added, 'I'm saying this because I badly want one myself.' Vasu barely swallowed the laughter that almost exploded in him.

'Does he never laugh?' He heard the girl ask his mother.

'You win,' he said, and taking a toffee, unwrapped it and put in his mother's mouth.

'Please take one, Mrs Sreenivasan, and put it in my mouth,' the girl told his mother, who did it willingly.

'And give him one. I think he had earned it.' His mother and the girl laughed, and the children joined in. She looked at him and said, 'Let your mother put one in your mouth, Mr Sreenivasan. Please. It will make the children so happy.'

He felt a bit foolish as his mother put a toffee in his mouth. There was loud clapping of hands, gurgles of laughter from the children, and the flashing of cameras.

'And now you are famous, and your pictures will be in all the social columns, and your chairman will read it,' she teased, as she led his mother back to her chair, and him to the stage.

'The agony is over,' she said rolling her eyes upwards.

Vasu's mother insisted on going with the girl to talk to some of the parents. It gave him so much satisfaction to see her, composed, elegant, so much at ease. And she seemed so friendly with the girl, less than half her age.

When they came back, his mother was telling her, 'You must visit us.'

'If you promise, your son will not throw me out,' she said, and his mother laughed. He had not heard her laugh with such girlish abandon before.

'I promise,' he snapped as he opened the car door for her.

'My mother thinks a bit better of me than you, or your clean-scrubbed children.'

'Oh, please keep the children out of this. I'm the culprit.' Her mood had suddenly changed. There was a desperate plea in her voice. 'And please don't spoil this wonderful evening I had with your mother, the children, and yes, with you.' Her face was turned towards him for a fleeting moment.

She just touched his mother's hand and briskly walked away. As they drove back, his mother was silent and withdrawn.

And later, when he was working on the product manager's report, she came into his room, and her voice was soft. 'Thanks son, for one of the best evenings I've had in a long time.' And before he could reply, she kissed him lightly on his forehead and walked quickly out of the room.

When Vasu came home a few days later, he found an oldish two-wheeler parked in the drive. He briskly stepped out of the car, and shouted, 'Mom, have the AC service chaps come?'

'No, the social service people are here,' said a familiar voice, and his mother was laughing with that children's home girl.

'Vasu, come here. I asked Roopa to tea. We've been waiting for you,' his mother called out.

'Not me. I wanted to flee. Mrs Sreenivasan wouldn't let me.'

'Now, Roopa, no more of this Mrs Sreenivasan stuff. And don't you Aunty me, just call me…'

'Amma?' came the unexpected reply. Her voice was so low, Vasu hardly heard her. 'I'm sorry if I startled you. My mother died years ago. You are so very much like her. But if you mind…'

'Mind? Oh no, my dear. I'd love you calling me Amma.' His mother put her hand on Roopa's arm.

'I hate to be sentimental, but you must know. Let me get it out and over. My Dad was in the civil service, and we were driving to Shimla for a holiday. My brother, back on vacation from the UK was at the wheel, with Dad beside him. My mother and I were in the back. We went head-on into a truck. Both Dad and my brother died right there. I was badly hurt, in a coma for days. My hips were almost crushed and had to be reconstructed. My mother was not too badly injured. But the shock… she had to be institutionalised and she just wasted away.'

'I'm so sorry,' his mother said, taking both Roopa's hands in hers. Vasu just kept looking at her. She had been so matter-of-fact, so direct. But her eyes were pools of anguish.

She turned towards him, and her mood seemed to change suddenly. He saw mischief twinkling in her eyes. 'I promise not to continue my sob story. Mr Sreenivasan is looking at me, as though he is seeing one of those dreadful tear-jerkers.'

His mother tried to smile.

'I'm really sorry,' he blurted out. 'For a moment, I just couldn't…'

'You didn't expect a girl coming here for the first time to talk so frankly. Isn't that true, Mr Sreenivasan?'

'Yes,' Vasu admitted.

'Thank you for being honest. But you know… something tells me this is not the first time I'm here with Amma and you. Please, please… believe me.'

Vasu and his mother exchanged a quick look. It did not miss Roopa. 'Now, please don't think I'm dotty. I know I've been here. It is for you to make what you will about this. And now, I think Mr Sreenivasan wants to relax, or rather to continue to work. So, in the interest of my safety, and the reputation of my sanity, I must depart.'

But his mother would have none of it, and soon they were at the dining table nibbling samosas hot from the kitchen, both chatting as though they had known each other all their lives. When she finally left, sweeping out of the drive on her moped, his mother turned to him, and her face seemed to glow.

Roopa's visits soon became frequent. One day, she took

his mother on her moped to the children's home. Vasu was furious. 'Mummy, how dare you go on a moped? That silly girl. What the hell does she think she is doing?' he snapped.

'But son, she is such a fine driver. And stupid as it may seem, it made me feel I was a girl once more. Even though my back is a bit stiff, sitting sideways on that narrow pillion.' She looked happier than he had seen her for long, and it silenced him.

Came the Sunday. He was keynote speaker at the Annual Convention of Pesticide Manufacturers. As usual, he asked his mother to go with him, and she said she would feel out of place if Roopa did not go, too. And so the three of them set out. Throughout the two-hour drive to the seaside hotel where the convention was being held, Vasu was so immersed rehearsing his presentation, he hardly heard them chatting in the rear seat.

It was in the auditorium that for the first time he looked at her closely. Roopa was graceful in a crisp orange cotton *sari*, her hair swept high to the back of her head. She was not the sort of girl one looked at feature by feature. But she was not a girl one could forget easily. It amused him that she had a scribble-pad on her lap and a pencil in hand. Throughout his presentation, she took notes, occasionally whispering to his mother. And during question time, her animated face turned from questioner to him, as though wishing him to do his best.

Once a challenging presentation like this to top-management was over, Vasu unwound fully. They walked barefoot to the beach from the seaside cottage allotted to them by their hosts. Vasu carried an icebox, with a couple of beers and soft drinks. Roopa had picked up some cushions. They sat on the sand like three picnickers, digging their toes into its warmth, and again Roopa startled them, 'Believe me, Amma, but I've been here with you before. Right here, sitting on the warm sand,' and her excited voice trailed away.

'And I sipped beer.' Vasu and his mother were amazed, and Roopa saw it. 'If you will not be scandalised, Mr Sreenivasan, can I sip a wee bit of beer from your bottle?' The switch in her mood was equally amazing.

'Now, Roopa,' said his mother. 'Be careful. Sip from the same bottle as Vasu, and you too will become an incurable workaholic. And now stop this Mr Sreenivasan stuff. He is Vasu, and she is Roopa to you, Vasu.'

'Just Roopa, not rope her,' Roopa retorted, and Vasu's mother was in stitches.

'Okay. It is Roopa from now on,' he said, admitting to himself he liked this strange girl, the way she talked, the way she dressed, even the sudden switch in her moods. And, above all the transparent honesty in all she said and did.

Roopa had become serious. 'You made out such a strong case for a more aggressive marketing strategy for pesticides, Vasu. But warning they were in the business of selling poisons, you said nothing about the future of this killing industry. Do you think it will survive? Can man kill cockroaches, and termites and bedbugs, bad as they are, without slowly killing mankind, and life itself, in the process?'

'I was just developing my presentation on "Marketing in the Decade of the Professional." Not talking about the ethics of marketing,' Vasu defended his paper.

'Can any activity, anything at all, and that includes marketing, ignore ethics?' she asked.

'No one asked this question. Why didn't you?'

'I thought you might think I was trying to be cheeky,' she said, 'Remember, I was a gatecrasher.'

'Oh no. The question is relevant. But all of us missed this point. I wish you had raised it. The discussions would have been so much more meaningful.'

'Thanks, Vasu, I think you are honest.' She said looking straight at him, 'I like honest people. There are so few of them around.'

His mother had leaned back on the cushions Roopa had propped up behind her, and they noticed that she was dozing. They fell silent, almost like conspirators. There was only the sound of the waves, and the swishing of palm fronds. Suddenly, he wanted to reach out to Roopa, touch her face, her hair, and hold her in his arms. Perhaps, she sensed this. She slowly rose, and walked away, leaving Vasu with his mother. And then Vasu knew he was in love with Roopa. He wanted to be with her now and always, and he wanted her as he had wanted no other girl, ever.

In a month, they were married.

It was as though Roopa had always been with them. She had been close to his mother from the time they met. Now, they did most things together. His mother regularly went to the children's home, where Roopa continued to work. Once, when Roopa was down with cold, he was surprised to know that his mother had gone by herself, to stand in for her. And with each passing day, he was deeper in love with this vivacious girl whom nothing seemed to faze.

He would wake in the morning, languorous with the ecstasy they shared the previous night, and reach out, to find her missing. She would be with his mother in the kitchen or garden, well groomed, immaculate in a housecoat.

She got his mother to tuck a rose in her hair. '*Appa* would have wanted you to do this. I know.' And then in that strange voice now increasingly familiar, 'I've seen you with a *ḅindi* on your forehead, your hair full of flowers. No, not in photographs, Amma. Really. I've seen you.'

These remarks perplexed Vasu. Once he asked her, and her answer was direct. 'You will not understand, Vasu. In my mind, events flash so clearly. Long before they actually happen. What happens, when it happens, seems in fact just a sort of replay.'

And answering his unasked question, 'No, I cannot explain. It was after the accident. You know I was in a coma for days. Since then, I get these flashes. At times, I can say for sure. Sometimes, it's all a bit hazy.'

She was not religious, never visited temples. There were no pictures of gods or gurus. Vasu never saw her pray. But she read books he had not heard of – on life after death, about ancient Buddhist monasteries, the lives of unknown mystics. At times, Vasu saw her eyes lift from a page and look far and away, as though she had drifted from him, from everyone. There was something other-worldly about her at these moments, and she made no attempt to hide it. Nor was she annoyed, when he sometimes intruded into these daydreams, as he chose to dismiss them.

And there certainly was nothing unworldly about her, when they were alone together. She could be atrociously demanding in bed, even shameless. She would walk into their room dripping from a shower, drying her wet hair, unselfconsciously proud of her firm, lovely body, eager to offer herself to him with a passion that endlessly seared him.

Once when Vasu was alone with his mother, he mentioned that Roopa could be rather unpredictable, and his mother said, 'You will never understand the depths in her, Vasu. I do. Believe me. She is firmly rooted. But she has not shut out other worlds we know nothing about.'

'Mom?'

'Let us not talk of her when she is not here,' was her reply.

When they had chanced on the subject, Roopa asked, 'How much do you really know about me, Vasu? No, I have no secrets to hide. Not from you, or Amma, or anyone else. What I'm talking about is my real self. If you can take a few days off, Amma and you could come to my village and spend a few days in my ancestral home, but then perhaps you would be bored, Vasu.'

At his mother's insistence they had motored down. Vasu was intrigued by the sprawling tiled mansion nestling in a large compound, full of trees, overgrown shrubs and flowering plants. Creature comforts, like hot running water, and modern toilets had been added. But everything else seemed to belong to a distant age. It was as though decade upon decade, maybe a hundred years of living, had left the place untouched.

Only a caretaker and his wife lived there. Chandu, dark and lean, always immaculate in a white short-sleeved vest and ankle-length dhoti, was the cook. His wife Cheeru, in the shirt-like blouse and checked lungis all the ladies there wore, did the washing and cleaning.

No, they had no children. Roopa was everything to them, they said. The old lady loved to comb Roopa's hair, and lace it with strange fragrant flowers. Sometimes, she would loop it like a bracelet round Roopa's wrist. They ate splendid food, with lots of fish, fruits, and greens, fresh from the compound.

One day, Vasu saw Roopa climb the steep wooden steps to a trap door in the ceiling.

'Roopa, what are you doing,' he called.

'Come and see for yourself,' and Vasu had climbed up too. They entered a very large tent-shaped attic, with long meshed ventilators on all sides. It was bare, but immaculately clean like the rest of the house.

'When Yogimaman was living here, the ventilators were open and this place was hardly ever swept. I can remember the cobwebs and sparrow's nests, with birds and squirrels darting in and out. He slept on a mat right here, in the middle of the room, with a brass water jug beside him. No one could say when he would come down. No one asked if he wanted anything. He just came and shared the food, or went into the compound and munched fruits and even leaves and twigs. There always was a strange fragrance about him, and deep in his smiling eyes a glint of fire. He must have been well into his eighties, but looked a sprightly sixty.' It was the first time Vasu heard about Roopa's uncle, Yogimaman. When he mentioned this, his mother said she knew.

'Yes, Vasu, I did keep it from you. I was afraid it may affect your marriage. You never believed these things, and there was no harm done. I knew you would get to know sometime, but by then Roopa would be a part of your life and mine. Roopa is no ordinary girl, Vasu. She is so many different persons. As a woman, I know marrying her is the best that could have happened to you.'

So many different persons! It kept repeating in his mind.

Roopa rolled over close one night, and with her face snug in the curve of his shoulder, murmured, 'Vasu, you are going to be a father.' And then to his surprise, was far more passionate than he had ever known.

The doctor confirmed the baby was on the way. She did a scan, and it showed the damage the car smash had done to Roopa's pelvic structure.

'I'm sorry to say this, Roopa, but with this damage, you will not be able to have your baby normally,' she said.

And later on to Vasu, 'Both for her sake and the baby's, it must be delivered only by Caesarean. Everything else is normal. The baby is fine. So is Roopa. But keep this in mind.'

They lived in a dream world from then. There was nothing Vasu's mother spared to please Roopa. As for Vasu, he was more deeply in love with her than ever before. He now skipped office Saturday noons. They drove to the beach, or sat on the lawns of the Boat Club. His mother always packed a splendid hamper, and as Vasu sipped beer,

Roopa tucked into the delicacies like a schoolgirl on a picnic.

Often in the night, when Roopa was asleep, he would prop himself on his elbow, and look at her, limp as a kitten, breathing ever so gently.

He teased her once, and she hugged him close, and said, 'Why should I care when you are beside me, Vasu? Only one thing makes me sad. When I think of Amma. For how many years, decades, has she slept all by herself, without the warmth, the smell, the passion of a man in bed. Sometimes, I wonder how I slept so many years in an empty bed without you, Vasu.'

For the first time, something he had sealed deep within him snapped. Vasu put his face on her breasts, and he wept like a child. She held him close, without a word. She did not even kiss him. But her silken body was warm, consoling. And then he made love to her with a tenderness she had never known before, almost as though she was a small child he was afraid he might hurt.

'The baby! Did I hurt you, my darling?' he asked.

'She must have just known how sweet her dad can be at times, and come out from some remote corner of my dysfunctional pelvis in which she must have hidden for safety in the past.' They both laughed.

'Shoo… Mom will hear, and she may be disturbed,' he cautioned.

'No Vasu, she must be asleep. We worked hard mowing the lawn today. She must be tired.'

'Mowing the lawn? In this condition?'he was astonished 'I must tell Mom…'

'Vasu, don't you dare,' Roopa flared. 'You have no idea, how much I love the work I share with Amma. She is like a girl when we work together. So full of fun, and laughter, and she takes such good care of me. Even my own mother wouldn't have given me so much love. And she tells me, that the more you work, the easier it will be when the baby comes. That is exactly what Yogimaman too used to say. The harder you work, the easier everything becomes.'

'There you go with your Yogimaman again.'

'Vasu, please don't let us get into this.' And she took his hand and pressed it on her belly.

'You see? She is kicking around there, knowing how naughty her Mom and Dad have been. But she also knows how much they love each other, and her too.'

She pulled his hands to her breasts, and her lips were wet and demanding, and this time their lovemaking was fierce, and then she wanted his whole weight on her, and when she fell asleep in his arms, Vasu knew he could not live without her. And he also knew, that when it came to Yogimaman, there was nothing he could do to change her total faith in him. He tried to pray. But he knew no prayers.

Since they always disagreed, they rarely talked about Roopa's Yogimaman. Vasu pieced together fragments of information like a jigsaw puzzle from small talk and casual comments.

From infancy, Yoganand had been different. Everyone seemed to treat him like a grown-up, listening carefully to what he said. It was not as though he was not childish or mischievous. He often played truant. But unlike other boys, he always helped his mother and servants in the kitchen, and helped clean and tidy the house, and even the courtyard. He drew water from the well for them, and helped wash soiled clothes, while other children frolicked.

The family was non-vegetarian, but Yogimaman had always been vegetarian. This used to worry his mother, but he was healthy, grew tall and was full of energy. He was also a very good student, though he spent little time with his books. He was always with his grandmother, who was deeply religious, and helped in the *poojas* she did, or listened to the scriptures she read aloud daily. Even on the most rainy day, he gathered flowers for her to decorate the prayer room.

What was striking was his love for animals and birds, indeed, all living creatures. Even when he swept the cobwebs, he had a knack of ensnaring spiders in the broom, and then freeing them in the compound. On the way to school, he was known to have often emptied his tiffin box before a stray dog. When he sat on the wall near the gate, dogs and cats would gather around, as though to keep him company.

'You will not believe this, Vasu,' Roopa once said. 'But when he was there, the most fierce dogs would not fight with cats. Squirrels would scamper across his shoulders.'

'I once had a squirrel for a pet, and it used to do this too,' Vasu quipped.

'But the mice. The rats?'

'Now, you are exaggerating, Roopa,' Vasu chided. 'Stories like this build up into fables.'

'I've not seen this, I agree. But my mother did, and my grandmother said she used to give him stale bread and biscuits for the rats. She herself told me this.'

'Fairy tales. Children love to hear stories and your grandmother must have spun a few yarns for a curious creature like you, just to keep you out of mischief.'

'Now Vasu…' his mother was annoyed, but Roopa just laughed.

'Could be possible, Amma,' she said in all seriousness. 'If I was in Vasu's place, I could have thought so myself.'

'But Vasu, you must try to understand what Roopa is trying to tell you…' his mother persisted.

Roopa had put her face against her shoulder, and kissed her hand when she caressed her cheek.

'Let him be, Amma, perhaps, he does not need to know all this. Yogimaman will bless him, and you – always. But for him, would I be here with both of you?'

'Oh! Come on now Roopa… What has he to do with this? You owe me to Mom,' Vasu teased.

'Yes, Vasu. To my Amma. To her…' and then her voice trailed away. 'But...but…'

'Yes, Roopa?' his mother prompted gently.

'You remember the day you came to the school, and distributed sweets?' Roopa asked, and her eyes pleaded with Vasu not to laugh.

'Can I ever forget that, Roopa?' his mother asked.

'You took a sweet and put it in my mouth…' she continued haltingly, '...and then, I can't say for sure, whether it was a dream, or a dream-wish…or just…just…,' she gave up when she saw Vasu's expression.

'Yes dear…' his mother urged gently.

It seemed her voice came from far away, from nowhere. But what she said was clear and sure. 'Yes, I saw Yogimaman standing next to you, Amma. And he smiled at me. He smiled at me, and he seemed so happy.'

A sharp glance from his mother silenced Vasu, as Roopa continued. 'I've wanted to tell Vasu this before, but I was afraid, Amma. Scared. I thought he would think I was out of my mind, and that I may lose him, and you.' And then she hid her face in his mother's shoulder, like a child seeking protection. His mother put her arm around her. Vasu was dumbstruck.

Later, when they were in bed, Roopa whispered, 'Vasu, please don't think I'm daft. I'm not. I don't even want you to believe all this. I only want to open my mind to you. One thing I want you to know. I love you. I will always love you. I can't live without you…'

In a surge of sympathy, Vasu held her close, and wiped the tears on her cheeks. 'Now go and wash your face,' he said. She went to the bathroom, and when she was back in bed, she drew his face down to her breasts, and even though Vasu was taut with passion, he lay still as she fell asleep still holding him to her bare breasts.

When he woke next morning, he could hear her vibrant voice in the kitchen, talking to his mother of a menu they were trying out for lunch.

Yoganand had excelled in school. He did well as a scout, and was nominated to represent the state at a parade. Tall, muscular and immaculately turned out, he had impressed the visiting officials, and the next thing his family knew was that he had enrolled in the Officers Training School. He was a Gentleman Cadet of his batch, winning the Sword for Excellence. He was commissioned into the Army.

Even though marriage proposals poured in for this handsome bachelor, he remained single. There was not very much more anyone knew about him, except that he had fought in the World War. All that Roopa knew was that when he came back, they found medals in a paper bag at the bottom of his box. He had been decorated for gallantry in action. It was said shrapnel got embedded in his throat and chest, which were removed only after a series of operations. And he sought discharge. From then, he lived in the attic almost withdrawing into a world of his own.

The rest was a blur. His love for animals and birds and even insects was a legend. It was said the temple elephant, would stop at his house and trumpet, till he came out and offered it plantains, or at least a handful of grass.

'I would do just that if I could get a free snack,' Vasu quipped.

'Perhaps, I too, Amma. Vasu's kidding does not upset me. But one thing for sure. Any person bitten by a snake, was brought to our house, and laid in the verandah. And in a few hours, the victim would be up and about, as though nothing had happened.'

'Without medication?' Vasu was sceptical.

'It is said, Yogimaman would not even come down from the attic at times. The cure just happened even if it was the most poisonous snake. People believed no one would die, once they were in that house. And now Vasu, stop that cynical smile, will you?'

'Sorry Roopa, I just cannot believe...' Vasu almost blurted crap, checked himself, and said, 'this sort of thing.'

'Vasu,' his mother snapped. He had never seen her so irritated.

'Amma, please.' Roopa pleaded, 'I'm not annoyed with Vasu. Anyone hearing this story could react exactly like this.'

It was not as though she was always so tolerant. She was furious the moment she saw children throwing stones at a dog, or bullocks yoked to an overloaded cart. The number of calls she made to the SPCA and Blue Cross became a constant family joke.

'Just remember Roopa, this is a company's phone,' he gently chided her once.

And when she next met his chairman at a party, she went up to him.

'Mr Sapru, Vasu says, I'm misusing your phone.'

'What do you mean, Roopa?' the chairman was surprised.

'I make a lot of calls to the Blue Cross, the SPCA, to my Home for Handicapped Children...'

'But Roopa, what are you trying to tell me?' he asked.

'Vasu says this is misusing company's facilities.'

'Ah ha!' Mr Sapru grunted, and then he called Vasu, 'Just a moment, young man. What is all this talk of misusing the company's phone?' he snapped.

'But Sir...'

'Keep your buts to yourself, Vasu. Let Roopa make as many calls as she wants.' And as Vasu stared daggers at Roopa, the chairman added, his eyes twinkling, as though he enjoyed this. 'I'm inclined to ask Roopa to sit in, when we next rate executive performance. If we have this sort of integrity in our company, I'd be really proud.'

When they got back from the party that night, Roopa went to his mother.

'Amma, do you think I was wrong?' she asked with the innocence of a ten-year old.

'You be just what you are, Roopa,' was all his mother said.

But when they were in bed, Vasu drew her close to him, and buried his face in her hair without saying a word. She clung to him.

'Darling. What would have happened to me had I not met you?' he whispered.

'Vasu, I thought I should tell your boss, as this seemed to be bothering you.'

Vasu suddenly pushed her away, sprang up on the bed, and saluted her.

'Okay, boss. Now, please don't cut my increment,' he pleaded. And they fell into each other's arms laughing, till his mother came into the room, and at Roopa's insistence Vasu had repeated his salute and plea, and his mother too laughed, holding her stomach, and almost collapsed on the bed.

'Come, we must celebrate the taming of the wild beast. Let's go to the kitchen and make black coffee, and Vasu can lace his with Cognac.'

'Me too,' said Roopa.

'Me too,' echoed his mother.

She was into her sixth month now. Preparations were afoot for the journey to Roopa's ancestral home. His mother and Roopa poured over check lists, and he caught snatches of their conversation…medicines, torches, sterilised cotton, and baby things like powder and feeding bottles and diapers.

Their doctor said this was sheer madness, and was astonished he allowed this. He would have to blame himself if he did not stop this, he warned. Vasu felt totally helpless, and said nothing. He got an oxygen cylinder.

'Amma, Vasu is all set for deep-sea diving,' laughed Roopa.

'Roopa, you must understand Vasu is doing what he thinks is best for you and the baby. The phone has already been connected, thanks to Vasu pulling strings all-around,' his mother chided her.

Vasu had bought a new jeep to negotiate the dirt roads in Roopa's village. He had it fitted with an extra wheel, and added a range of tools and spares to the kit. He had found a folding wheelchair, that could double as a lean-back stretcher, and lock between the rear seats.

'Vasu, what are you doing, dear?' Roopa seemed amused. 'What is all this for? If I felt I would need all this, wouldn't I have stayed on here, and checked into that plush five-star hospital, where everyone springs to attention at the sight of you?'

The jeep and a rented car, sent earlier, were at the airport when they flew into the airport, two hours by road to Roopa's village. Throughout the flight and drive, Roopa chattered like a child going home for holidays after exams.

But as they pulled into the compound, Roopa leaned forward, her hands gripping his shoulders. 'I have seen this before.' Her voice was clear and loud. 'Everything, including the jeep. I have even heard its wheels churning gravel.' And as usual, her voice trailed, and was lost in a whisper.

A moment later, she was different, saying, 'With you around Vasu, the gates will be oiled, greased, and will stop creaking.'

His mother said nothing, her face drawn and tired. Vasu just stared ahead, his jaw jutting even more stubbornly.

'If only it was raining,' Roopa bubbled. 'The whole place gets that clean-scrubbed look after a spell of rain.'

And makes things disastrous, thought Vasu. The road, particularly the causeway, could flood, and you would then hardly get through. He had worked out a meticulous schedule. He had to get back to the site office to complete final touches to the major project the company had taken up. After the MoU was initialled by their Board and their collaborators, he had leave to stay a whole month with Roopa. With the telephone link, he could keep in touch.

Once they had settled down, Vasu could not remember happier days with Roopa. She had brought their two-in-one. Early mornings, when the slanting rays of the sun streamed in, he would wake leisurely to the lilting music of the instrumental tapes she had brought.

Vasu asked her why she did not play them in their home in the city.

'Roopa thinks it will disturb you. We use my Walkman and listen in kitchen or garden when we work,' his mother said.

'Music like this belongs to nature, to silence, to unhurried ways, Vasu,' Roopa said, 'To beauty, to peace like this.'

'Oh! come on Roopa,' he chided.

But she drifted away, and he barely heard her. 'What a heavenly place for our child to be born.' Vasu and his mother could not take their eyes off her. She seemed to glow and was so lovely!

Vasu was always worried when he saw Roopa climb the steep, narrow wooden steps to Yogimaman' s attic, her belly scraping the steps as she went up.

'I'm just going up to make sure I'm safe.' She was serious.

'Yogimaman would like to see me, and her too,' she smiled, tapping her belly.

Vasu had long realised there was no point in arguing. Deep within he was coming to know, she was in many ways a different person. His mother who knew her better than him in this respect, seemed to understand, without really knowing what it was.

'She is like most girls, Vasu. They completely shut out part of themselves from everyone. But it often is some ugly, some unpleasant secret they want to hide. With Roopa, it's different. She seems to have, what shall I say, a sort of link with this uncle, who she feels is a saint. You just can't explain it. Words are not enough. Nor arguments. You have to learn to live with it, Vasu.'

'Mom, but at what price? By…'

'Vasu,' she had snapped.

'Okay, Mom Okay. But dammit, I'm sorry, Mom. Sometimes, I feel so helpless. I'm afraid things are getting completely out of control.'

'How many things in life are really within our control, Vasu?' she asked, and she too seemed to speak from far away.

Vasu looked at her. He saw in her face, the lines that had cut in, and each seemed to etch the years of agony after she had lost his father. He put his arms around her, and they stood there, mother and son, with just an unspoken prayer in their hearts.

After it was all over Vasu could never put the bits and pieces together to get a clear picture. The work with the visiting delegation had all but finished, and in a day, they would have signed the agreement. Vasu had already told his chairman, that he would like to leave immediately, to be with Roopa.

As usual, he called Roopa in the morning.

'Everything okay,' she told him. 'Just one little bother. Vijay the driver, is down with suspected enteric, and has been hospitalised. I have sent the nurse to make sure he is cared for properly.'

'Good gracious,' Vasu exploded. 'Who is there to drive

the jeep?'

'There is no need for anyone right now, Vasu. So, why worry?' But he was already planning to fly down a standby driver the next morning.

'I saw the TV weather forecast. Predicts rain along the west coast. That's worrying,' he said.

'It is a bit cloudy, Vasu, but there is no trace of rain. I can't wait for it to rain. It makes this place blossom,' Roopa was cheerful.

'But Roopa, no driver, and if the rains come…'

'You always think of worst case scenarios, darling.'

His mother sounded apprehensive. 'I've asked Chandu to try and find a driver,' she said. 'We need a driver here. I've also alerted the doctor.'

So far, so good. But when Vasu got through to the airline the next morning, to confirm the driver's ticket, he was told that due to bad weather there were no flights that day.

They were signing the Memorandum of Understanding the next morning, and he told the chairman, that he would like to catch the train in the evening.

They had just finished signing the MoU, when his mother came on the line, and in an anxious voice told him that Roopa was developing what would seem to be early pains. And it was raining, and no, they had yet to find another driver. Vasu almost froze with fear. In an hour, he had organised two cars. When he rang to inform his mother he was starting, the telephone lines were dead.

It had begun as a mere drizzle, but the rains seemed to keep pace with Roopa's pains. Soon, it was a steady downpour, and then it worsened into a mild storm. As early as three in the noon, the skies darkened, and the winds thrashed the trees. Chandu and his wife closed the windows, but were unperturbed.

Roopa's behaviour amazed Vasu's mother. She could see

the girl wince as pains struck, but she stood near the large window, enjoying the storm, now raging with increasing fury.

'Roopa…,' she tried to hide the panic that choked her.

'Amma, please don't worry. Yes, I think the pains have started. It's two to three weeks premature,' Roopa said calmly.

'But who is there to get the doctor. He wouldn't even know.' Vasu's mother was scared now.

'You are here, Amma, and Chandu and Cheeru, and then…' Roopa hesitated, as though she did not want to continue. But Vasu's mother did not miss her fleeting look at the trap-door in the ceiling.

Then, everything seemed to blur. Roopa's pains quickened. Even though she bit her lips, she moaned, and her hands clutched her belly. In the crash of thunder, they did not hear the doctor's car squeal into the portico. He had brought the nurse and a theatre boy with him.

'This is some weather,' he shouted, as he dashed into the house. Soon, they were all in Roopa's room, and Vasu's mother heard the rattling of surgical instruments. Cheeru was boiling water in the kitchen.

And then she was drawn, as though in a trance, to the steep steps that led to the attic. She went up in a daze, one step at a time. She did not know how to open the trap-door, and she was afraid to loosen her grip on the steps. So, she slowly pushed it up with her head. She barely got it open, and she could not remember if she saw a glow in the middle of the room, or was it just another flash of lightning? How long she stood there, she did not know. She could not also recall coming down. But when she was back on the floor, there was total silence in the room where the doctor and nurse were with Roopa. Her legs were so heavy she could hardly move.

And then there was a blinding flash of lightning, and

only the howling of the wind, before the ear-splitting crash of thunder, And with it, the happiest sound ever, the cry of a new born, clear, loud, almost as though it wanted to be heard above the fury of the storm.

She rushed to the room, and the doctor looked over his shoulder, 'Just a moment, Mrs Sreenivasan, and you can see your granddaughter,' he said cheerfully.

Her head began to spin and she collapsed against the doorpost.

It had stopped raining by the time Vasu reached. He came charging up the steps, hair tousled, face ashen, his wet shirt half out of his soaked folded-up trousers.

'You want to see your daughter?' his mother asked him, and hand in hand they entered Roopa's room. Cheeru was sitting on the floor, the baby cosy in her lap. Roopa's face beamed when she saw him, and a tear trembled on her eyelash.

'Vasu, don't tell me you drove through that storm?' she asked in a faint voice.

Vasu had a lump in his throat. He tried not to cry, and as was his wont, decided to be angry instead. 'I told you… I told you…' and then he could say nothing more.

Roopa raised a tired arm, and rubbed her fingers against his stubble and jabbed his nose.

'Ruffian,' she said, with a wan smile.

Vasu reached out and gently touched the baby in Cheeru's lap. Then, he turned, and kneeling, buried his face against his mother, and he cried, as she stroked his hair, and spoke things she would to a frightened child.

When the doctor came the next morning, the sky had cleared. The early morning sun lit up the rain-washed greenery. Vasu was immaculate in cream kurta-pyjamas.

'Hello Vasu, I knew you would come one way or other. Happy about the little girl? She is just a couple of weeks premature. All the better, because she could come more easily.'

Vasu was silent. He just looked at Roopa.

Later when they all sat around, chatting over tea, the doctor said, 'It's good you sent that old chap to fetch me. The main road was flooded, but he knew the bypass, and we came through. I drove down the main road this morning. Just managed to get through. It's still under almost a foot of storm-water.'

Mrs Sreenivasan tried to speak, but a slight sign from Roopa silenced her.

'Though, how he waded through, and reached my home in such nasty weather I can't imagine. He is a gutsy chap for his age, to have made that trip.' The doctor continued, looking directly at Chandu.

All of them were quiet. Chandu did not understand as the doctor spoke in English. He left with the empty cups.

'And now I must be off,' the doctor said. Vasu went with him.

'Things have worked out somehow or other, Vasu,' he told him before he started the car. He put it in gear and moved, then braked. He hesitated for a moment. 'Vasu, people believe that even if a person bitten by a poisonous snake is brought here, he will pull through. But tell Roopa not to stretch her luck this much in future.'

Vasu kept mulling over this as he walked back to the house. For that matter, how did he manage to reach the house? The road was flooded, and the driver had waded a few steps and scrambled back, saying that the fierce swirl of the mountain stream would sweep away the car. And then there was this chap in an olive green cap and mackintosh, and he asked where are you going in this weather, and when Vasu told him, 'Oh! the Yogi's place, he said, 'I'll show you the other route.'

Later in the day, he took Chandu aside, and asked him about the other route.

'Which other route?' the old man asked.

'Oh! nothing. I just asked,' Vasu said.

Life now revolved around the baby. Vasu always thought of babies as a nuisance. But his daughter was so good-natured, she hardly ever cried. Vasu loved to see Roopa feed her. Droplets of her milk trickled on the baby's cheek, and sometimes inflamed him with a passion he was ashamed of.

Roopa saw this and drew him close when she was feeding the baby one day. 'She's a real menace like you, Vasu.' And to his surprise, she had pulled his face down to her other breast, and with a furtive glance at the door, to make sure there was no one around, offered it to him. Unthinkingly he leaned forward, and suddenly his mouth was full of the sweet warmth that flowed from her.

'She's competing with you, Vasu,' Roopa teased, ruffling his hair.

'Wait till we get back home...' Vasu warned as he kissed her gently.

'Home?' she asked vaguely. And she suddenly seemed far away, deep in that inner world of hers, 'Home?' she whispered.

'Darling, we are not going to stay here forever, are we? In two weeks, we'll be back. I've booked train tickets for a leisurely journey.'

'Journey?' she asked, still very remote.

'Now Roopa,' Vasu could not keep the edge out of his voice.

'Oh! Vasu, I'm so sorry. Now what did I say to annoy you so much?' She asked to his surprise.

As the day they were to leave approached, Roopa again showed signs of an increasing vagueness.

'Vasu, will you let me go up into Yogimaman's attic just once?'

Vasu hesitated, 'If the doctor will allow you, Roopa...'

The doctor said, why not? She had a normal delivery, and if she wants to go up a few steps, and Vasu was there to help, certainly.

And so the next day, Vasu had followed her up those steep steps. He climbed, his body against her back, his arms shielding her from both sides as they went up a step at a time.

Once in the room, Roopa was a different person, 'Oh! Vasu, how wonderful to be here with you, all by ourselves in Yogimaman's room, our very own room!' And suddenly she pulled down his head and kissed him with a passion that was demanding, biting his lips, his tongue. Vasu had to fight down the passion that flooded him.

He picked her up in his arms, and she said, 'Let us stand in the middle of the room for a while, my dearest.'

He never knew how long he stood there, with Roopa in his arms, her arms tight around his neck. They were startled by his mother's voice from below.

'Now, what are you two doing up there? Vasu, why did you allow Roopa to go up?'

They came down almost like naughty children. Vasu had never seen his mother so angry.

'Roopa,' she snapped.

Roopa stepped forward, and kneeling at his mother's feet, put her arms around her, burying her face in her lap.

'Roopa darling, I did not want to scold you. I was so worried, I could not help it,' his mother's voice quavered.

But Roopa continued to cling to her till Vasu leaned down, and helped her back to her feet. His mother kissed her on both her cheeks.

From then, Roopa seemed a different person. She was excited, about getting back, humming as she went about her packing.

But Vasu noticed that her hands lingered on all she touched. The pillars, the doors, the bedsteads, the backs of chairs, and even the walls. Increasingly, she chose to squat on the wooden steps to the attic, resting her head on its sides.

'We are not leaving for ever, are we, Roopa?' Vasu teased. 'I for one want to come back. I've never enjoyed myself more, sleeping late, lazing about, watching you feed that ever-hungry brat.'

'Can I ever forget this house?' his mother was wistful. 'Chandu, Cheeru...and that the baby came here.'

It slowly dawned on them, that Roopa never said anything when they talked of coming back.

'I hope this has not been traumatic for her,' Vasu confided in his mother when Roopa was away having a bath.

'I don't know, Vasu...' She admitted, 'But in some strange way, Roopa seems to have changed.'

'Mom?' there was no answer, except a puzzled, worried look.

Roopa came in with Cheeru, and sat on the bed as the old lady briskly towelled her hair.

'And now let me bathe the baby,' Cheeru said.

'No. Amma will do that,' Roopa told her. For the first time, Vasu saw Cheeru upset, and she left the room in a huff. When she came back to say that the water had been warmed, Roopa went up to her and put her arms around her, holding the old lady close.

'I said that only because you will not be there to bathe the baby when we get back,' she said. 'Let her get used to Amma. You just help her.' The old lady nodded, and was all smiles again. She clung to Roopa for a moment.

Let her get used to Amma! Why did those words keep echoing in his mind?

Everything was packed. Chandu carried them to the verandah, arranging them neatly for loading into the vehicles. His mother, with Cheeru carrying the baby, was in the verandah, and Vasu was directing the drivers to back the vehicles into the portico.

They were stunned by a deafening crash in the house. Vasu sprinted into the drawing room, shouting 'Roopa... Roopa... where are you?'

It took a while for the dust to settle. And through the haze, he saw that the trap-door in the ceiling had caved in, ricocheted down the wooden steps, and lay splintered on the floor. Some steps had also snapped, and the entire staircase tilted slightly to one side.

'Roopa,' he called again, his voice in chorus with his mother's. She had also come running into the room. 'Roopa,' he shouted, choked by panic at the thought that she could have gone up to the attic on her own. He heard a faint rustle behind him, and spun round. Roopa was crouching against the wall, staring at the ugly socket that stared down at them.

Her expression startled him. It was not fear, not even shock. She seemed entranced by what she saw through that gap in the ceiling. Her head had drooped slightly backwards. Slowly, she held out both her arms, palms upturned in pathetic helplessness. Or, was it defeat? Her lips were moving, and Vasu barely caught the words... 'gone... gone.'

He put his hands on her shoulders, and shook her gently. She looked at him and whispered 'Vasu', pointing at the ceiling.

Seeing her safe, he was himself again. 'Chandu,' he snapped, 'Get the drivers. Let us clear up this mess. Quickly. There is not much time. We have a train to catch.'

There was a flurry of activity, as the four of them removed the debris. His mother took the child from Cheeru, who joined them, and soon the room was dusted and swept clean.

'Now, let us get going real fast,' Vasu ordered, 'Or else

we miss the train, and will be right back here.' He led Roopa to the car, and without looking back she followed his mother into it. She did not take leave, or even wave to Chandu or Cheeru as they drove away.

It was only when they were out of the gate that she turned to Vasu. 'Thanks for helping to clean up the place,' she said. And then closed her eyes and leaned back on the seat.

'I'll send down some chaps to fix the stairway and the trap-door as soon as we get back,' Vasu told her, but she did not seem to hear.

Within minutes of boarding the train, Vasu had everything organised. Chandu and Cheeru had packed a marvellous dinner, and Vasu had not forgotten to fill his hip flask. Roopa too seemed her normal self again. They ate well, and then Roopa fed the baby, till she fell asleep in her arms.

'Amma, can she sleep with you? ' Roopa asked.

'Why ask, my dear?' His mother moved to make place for the baby.

Vasu sat on Roopa's berth, his arm around her. She snuggled against his shoulder. They watched his mother and the baby on the berth opposite. The rocking of the train had lulled his mother to a doze, but her hand rested protectively on the baby's knees.

'She is so safe... so safe with Amma.' Roopa whispered as she rubbed her face against Vasu's shoulder. 'With Amma, she will always be safe.'

Vasu turned off the bright neon lights. He had already drawn the jaded curtains around their berths. They sat close together, like lovers sharing a precious moment that could be snatched away any moment.

'She is so safe,' Roopa repeated softly, with a deep sigh of contentment. Vasu swallowed the lump in his throat. He could imagine himself as a baby, snug against his mother. What went through her mind every time the baby lay beside her, he wondered.

The speeding train seemed to float timelessly, locking the three of them together. If only it could always be like this, Vasu wished. But no, he could not shake off the thought, that each of them, so close, so inseparable, was in fact, sealed into completely different worlds. It frightened him, and he drew Roopa closer to him.

She brushed her lips against his arm, and hesitantly pushed him away. He tucked her in, and saw her faint smile as his hands lingered on her warm breasts. He kissed his mother lightly on her head, and touched the satin smoothness of the baby's ear lobe, before he swung himself to his berth above his mother's. He lay still, soaking in the cosiness of this tiny world, all his own.

And then it came back to him with snapshot precision. The haze through which he saw the splintered trap-door, the broken steps and the tilt of the staircase. How many times had they gone up those steep steps – Roopa by herself, the two of them together. His mother, too. He was vexed with himself for not having checked out its soundness earlier. If it had…

He shook himself free, pushing it away into the past, as he had put away Roopa's decision to come out here, the way the baby came. He forced himself to think of the delight of life ahead, Roopa, the baby, his mother, and the challenge of the project awaiting him. But no, thoughts of Roopa's Yogimaman started cutting in, throwing into sharp focus, so much he had dodged so long.

Smiling beside his mother on that fateful day in the children's Home, Roopa had said. How he had ridiculed her later. His mother's incredible account of climbing those steep steps and pushing open the trap-door with her head. What drove her to this unbelievable folly? Thanks Amma, Roopa said, and it seemed she had said much. And then, who had alerted the doctor and got him home that nasty night? Certainly not, Chandu. And grudgingly, how did he manage to ford the perilous mountain swirl that hurtled across the road. It could have swept away even a lorry!

Annoyed with himself, he tried to sit up, and hit his head against the ceiling. He propped himself on his elbow and looked down. In the eerie bluish purple of the night lamp, it was as though he was seeing the three he loved most in the world through an underwater porthole. Each so clearly visible, so utterly lovely.

But why then a strange radiance around Roopa? And why was it fading away? Had he fallen asleep? Was he dreaming? Why the wild hooting of the engine's siren? The piercing screech of metallic brakes? The deafening clash of metal all-around? And why suddenly this inky darkness? Was he really flung out of his berth like a paper toy? Why were the boxes he had so neatly stacked under the seats crashing on him?

He found himself thrashing about in a frenzy, straining to shake himself out of this nightmare. But it didn't seem to go away. He kept flaying his arms, groping, searching, clawing. He had to reach his mother. And the baby, where was she? He struggled, fighting the waves of exhaustion that swept over him. He lost count of time.

From far away the faint sounds of crowbars pounding metal, hollow bell-like chimes echoed in the darkness. He pushed, pulled, dragged himself free, till he felt a wall, and then thank heavens, the edges of the sealed-in glass window of the AC compartment. His groping hands found the grip of a smallish suitcase. Putting all he had into it, he smashed the box against the window, once, twice, and heard the glass splinter. He glimpsed the icy-blue spurt of an oxyacetylene flame turn in his direction, followed by the blinding sweep of arc lights.

The crowbars were pounding close now, and he heard the

steel window-guards being ripped away. He tried to swing the box once more, but was too weak even to lift it. His voice failed when he tried to shout. Or was it smothered in sobs?

Suddenly, there were voices, many voices. And with it a glimmer of hope, and one last surge of energy. He heard a moan, and someone rolled towards him. He pushed, heaved the body through the smashed window. Then, he blacked out.

When he came to, he found himself on a hospital bed. It had not been a nightmare after all.

'The baby?' The feeble voice he heard was his.

'Safe. Not a scratch. Your mother had protected her with her body.'

An icy foreboding closed around him. He shut his eyes, refusing to think. They must have thought he had fainted. He heard someone say his mother too was safe.

Much later, they wheeled him into Roopa's room, but he could see only her face. She was shrouded in white. Her body had been crushed, and she must have died instantly.

Across the room, he saw his mother, also in a wheelchair. She wept silently, her tears dropping into her lap. The nurse behind her, carrying the baby, was weeping, too.

Though he ached all over, he leaned to put his face against Roopa's. It was icy cold.

And then all he remembered was carrying her in his arms in Yogimaman's attic, her arms tight around his neck, as he swirled her in the centre of the room.

Why, oh why, had they come down those steep steps?